The *X* man was no longer her responsibility. She was not responsible for every two-bit scumbag and drugged-out skinhead in New York City. She was out. She was finally out. Out of the fighting game. Out of the vigilante justice game. She was free. Free to fall in love and have a relationship and a family like everybody else. Free to run for her goddamn life. Just like everybody else.

And that was just what she did. She took off with every ounce of strength and speed she had in her and ran for her life.

Don't miss any books in this thrilling series:

FEARLESS™

Available from SIMON PULSE

FEARLESS™

NORMAL

FRANCINE PASCAL

SIMON PULSE
New York   London   Toronto   Sydney

First Simon Pulse edition January 2004

Copyright © 2004 by Francine Pascal

Cover copyright © 2004 by 17th Street Productions,
an Alloy company.

SIMON PULSE
An imprint of Simon & Schuster Children's Publishing Division
1230 Avenue of the Americas, New York, NY 10020

Produced by 17th Street Productions,
an Alloy company
151 West 26th Street
New York, NY 10001

Fearless™ is a trademark of Francine Pascal.

Printed in the United States of America
10 9 8 7 6 5 4 3 2 1

Library of Congress Control Number: 2003108407
ISBN: 0-689-86706-9

To Johanna Stokes

I don't have any cold, hard statistics to back this up, but I think it's safe to assume that at one point or another, everyone must become pretty damn sick of themselves.

I mean, honestly, how could this *not* happen? How could people *not* grow dizzyingly, violently sick of themselves after a while? Because what are we really talking about here? We are talking about twenty-four hours a day, seven days a week. That's how much time we are forced to spend with ourselves, sleeping, eating, talking, fighting, dressing, undressing—it never stops.

I have spent *every waking moment* of my life with me. And the truth is. . . I am sick to death of it.

I can't really fathom who, in their right mind, would *not* be sick of me at this point. My life, after all, never seems to change. Well, it did: Ella died; Mary died; Loki ceased to exist.

But really, it didn't: Natasha appeared; Tatiana appeared; Yuri came back from the dead. My life really just repeats itself over and over in this dismal cycle: tragedy. . . then hope. . . then something very closely resembling actual happiness, and then—without fail—tragedy again. I'm a tragicomic broken record—a study in numbing emotional monotony. I'm one very long sad-ass story that *never* seems to end.

Until now.

Now I am stating it for the record. If I could scream it to this entire pain-in-the-ass city, I would. If I could take out an ad in every piece-of-crap paper in New York, I would do it. Because I want everyone who has ever known me to hear this and to understand it:

I am hereby changing my life. I am breaking the cycle. I am breaking it here and now and forever, because I can—because for the first time in God knows how long, I think I have a real

chance to do it. I have the
pieces of a real life staring me
in the face, and I swear to God,
I am going to put them together
if it kills me.

I have a father. I have an uncle
I can trust. My enemies are gone:
Yuri, Natasha, Tatiana. . . . I
have a *brother*—a *real* brother. And
I have this boy. . . Jake. I don't
even know what we are yet, but I
refuse to screw it up. I have a
chance to do it *right* this time.
All of it. A chance to be *real*—a
real girl with real feelings—no
matter how pathetic I might end up
looking, no matter how embarrassing
my complete emotional ineptitude
might be at first.

A new beginning. That is what I
have here. That is what this is
going to be for me. A new beginning with a new Gaia. A Gaia who
doesn't bitch and moan about her
existential woes. A Gaia who
doesn't repeat the same fatalistic
routine over and over again. A
Gaia who doesn't have to be nause-
atingly sick of herself anymore.

I've already been given my
first test.

The Agency has sent my father
off on another assignment.

Already.

I had him safe and sound back
home for a piddling couple of
weeks, and now he's already been
called away again to oversee some
big hush-hush op in Syria.

Now, *old* Gaia would be ranting
about this already—launching into
the same old orphan sob story.
But I am not going to be that
Gaia anymore. I'm not. I'm just
going to recognize the facts for
what they are: My father is a
high-ranking agent in the CIA.
This is his job. And if he needs
to leave on another mission, so
be it. I'm not going to cry about
it. And we've already agreed: I'm
not going to live in that
Seventy-second Street apartment
while he's gone. No way. Not
without him there. Those kinds of
hideously lonely days are over.

So I've agreed to stay in some
kind of boardinghouse downtown. I

guess it's some kind of CIA safe
house where kids of agents can
stay while their parents are on
assignment. The only other thing I
really know about the place is
that it's run by a Japanese
governess named Suko Wattanabe.
Apparently my father knew her back
in his intensive martial arts
training days. Whatever. At least
I'll be downtown again—free from
the horrifically bland shackles of
the Upper East Side, back in the
real world where there are actually people with ages and incomes
under sixty-five.

    Jake's going to help me move
my stuff into the boardinghouse
tonight, and that will be that.
No bitching about another foster
home or being left with
strangers. *No more bitching,
period.* Because I am so sick of
it. I am sick to death of the
half-assed, violent, depressive
soap opera that's been shoved
down my throat for the last five
years. It's not a life. I'm not
even sure what you would call

what's been passing for my life.
I think you'd call it "God's
cruel joke." And I don't even
believe in God.

It doesn't matter. The point
is, I'll tell God or the Fates or
anyone else who wants to listen:

The joke is officially over. I
am pressing reset. *Do over*. I am
starting my life again.

No one was
going to be
scared of
that **bizarro**
bitch
anymore. **world**
Now it was
her turn to
be scared.

MALCOLM COULD TASTE THE CITY DIRT

on his tongue. Dry weeds and raw sewage. Disgusting. Another morning after in Washington Square Park...

Finding God

Not morning like those 1 A.M. sweaty Egg McMuffin mornings, but morning like *real freaking morning*. Dawn. Everything was just starting to light up in sharper and sharper lines, turning from that weird comic-book blue to pasty gray.

Malcolm sat up on the grass and kicked Devin's pale, skinny ass to wake him up.

"Dude," he uttered, hawking up a night's worth of smokes and spitting at Devin's feet. "Get the hell up, dude, it's five-thirty." He smacked his watch until it stopped beeping in his ear. "*Goddamn* it, I told you we'd pass out. If we missed him, I'm gonna pound you, I swear."

Devin kicked him back in the leg and then dragged himself up to a sitting position, rubbing his bony fingers over his stubbly shaved head. "We didn't miss him," he said. "Five-thirty. You can only find him at five-thirty."

Last night's stink was pouring off of them both, penetrating Malcolm's pierced nostrils with the rank odor: spilled beer on his jeans from his last forty, the burnt taste of the crappy weed they'd smoked. He remembered about a quarter of the night. They'd ripped off some NYU bitches in the park. He'd beaten the crap out of some Chelsea asshole at CB's who'd had a problem with his swastika earring, and then they'd spent the rest of the night just looking for some decent E. All they'd gotten was crap. Total bunk. Children's aspirin and some Tylenol Cold with a smiley face punched into it. He'd been just about ready to cram his knife right through the last dealer's gut when they ran into Max.

And that's when Max told them about *him*.

Max swore that he'd met the guy. For real. He swore that it wasn't just a rumor being spread around by the brotherhood and every other skeevy lowlife in the park.

"I'm telling you, dude, this is no bull," Max had promised. "He'll be there. At five-thirty. He'll be sitting on the bench by the MacDougal Street entrance. He's got spiky blue hair. Blue shades. Real cold and calm. Like a ghost or something. But don't get spooked. Here's what you gotta say to him: You gotta say, 'Bless me Father, for I have sinned. I want to pray.' Then you gotta say, 'I don't want to be afraid anymore.' And if you do it right, he'll hook you up. And it's *cheap*, yo. Five doses of Invince for fifty bucks."

"You're so full of crap," Malcolm had argued. "Invince is such a lie."

"No, dude. This is for real. This is realer than real. Five-thirty A.M. Western entrance. That's the only time he's there. That's the only time you can find God."

Malcolm would have laughed right in Max's face except the truth was, he had seen what the stuff could

9

do—at least what everyone was saying it could do. He and Dev had both seen it. It was like E times ten. It was like super-E or something. Only it was better than that. It was more than a high. He'd seen a few of the other skinheads trip out on the stuff like they were goddamn superheroes, `like they were bullet-proof` or something.

Mal had to get a taste of IV. He had to. And not just for the rush. No, he had another reason. *Revenge.* Revenge for what she had done to his cousin and to half the other brothers, too. He knew they would all back him up on his plan.

But first things first. It was all just a fantasy until he and Devin could find him. It was time to find God.

Malcolm shook the grass and dirt off the T-shirt he'd used as a pillow and stretched it over his tattooed chest. "Come on," he said, flicking the back of Devin's neck to get him moving.

They strode through the park, their combat boots crunching the dead grass and then clomping on the barely sunlit pavement. Mal kept an eye out for cops, but there was really no need. Everybody knew `they didn't sweep the park for assholes until six.`

They started to close in on the MacDougal Street entrance, nearing the third bench on the path. . . .

And goddamn if he wasn't sitting right there. Malcolm could still only see him from the back, but that was all he needed to see.

This was the guy. The one and only "God." His shock of spiky blue hair reflected the grayness of the morning. His long arms were spread out like an eagle's wings across the back of the bench, a thick silver bracelet on each wrist. He sat completely still, like a washed-out photograph or a painting. It was just like Max had said. He was like a ghost. . . .

Malcolm and Devin both held up about six feet away, though Malcolm didn't know why. No, that wasn't true. He knew why. He was scared. At least he could admit it to himself, even if he'd never say it out loud to Dev. Even from six feet away, God was freaking creepy. There was just no denying it.

But that was exactly why Malcolm wanted the stuff, wasn't it? He wanted to kill that feeling. He wanted to feel totally invincible. Even if only for a couple of hours. That was the plan. That was how he'd finally get his revenge—how they would all get their revenge on that blond bitch.

They stood there staring at the back of God's head.

"Is that him?" Devin whispered.

"Of course it's him." Malcolm rolled his eyes and lit the last bent cigarette from the crumpled pack in his pocket. "Who the hell else could it be?"

"Hey! Are you God?" Devin called out.

Malcolm jabbed him hard in the ribs. "Shut the *hell* up, asshole!" he whispered.

"What?"

"That's not what you *say*. Don't screw this up. I want that *stuff*."

"Well, so do I—"

"Then *shut up*."

Malcolm shoved Devin back two steps. He stubbed out his cigarette with his boot and then gazed at the back of God's head. He took a deep breath and then he forced out the words. "Bless me, Father, for I have sinned. . . . I—I want to pray. . . ."

God's head did not move, nor did his arms.

"Dude, this is total bull—"

"Wait," Malcolm snapped, shutting Devin up. He turned back to face God's deadly still body. "I, uh. . . I don't want to be afraid anymore. . . ."

Silence filled the edge of the park. And then God's head finally began to turn. He turned his head about fifteen degrees, and he spoke. He spoke in a hushed and measured baritone.

"Sit with me," God said calmly.

Malcolm and Devin began to approach, but God stopped them.

"Just the one," he insisted.

They froze in place. Malcolm glimpsed Devin and then began his solo approach, moving even more slowly this time. The closer he got, the farther away he wanted to be. But finally he managed to sit down at the end of the bench, trying not to stare too long at God's profile or his blue shades, which were just starting to pick up the first real glints of orange sunlight.

They sat for a moment in silence. Malcolm tried to steady his shaky leg.

"God. . ." He puffed out a nervous laugh. "That's, uh. . . that's a ballsy name for a dealer."

God turned slowly and faced him dead-on. "You obviously haven't tried this stuff yet," he said. He reached into his pocket and presented a blue cellophane package that fit in the palm of his hand. "Fifty gets you five. One for ten."

"I need ten."

"I thought you might." God slid the package across the bench and Malcolm trapped it under his finger-tips. There were ten small diamond-shaped yellow pills inside. Then he handed God the hundred bucks from inside his boot.

Thank you, rich NYU bitches.

"D-Does it. . . ?" Malcolm stammered. "Does it really work? I mean, if, like, some. . . *dude* and. . . his whole gang had been beating the crap out of me and my boys for a while, you know. . . messing with us in our own park. . . ? Would we be able to—?"

"That dude wouldn't stand a chance," God said. "It wouldn't matter how big his gang was. You drop one of these, and you won't care if an armored tank is coming at you."

"Sweet," Malcolm said, trying for a moment to bond with God. But he didn't even need to see God's

13

eyes behind those blue shades. He knew he should shut up instantly. Shut up and go.

"Tell your people," God said. "Tell them to come and pray while supplies last."

"I will," Malcolm said. "Totally." He looked back at Devin, waved the package, and grinned.

Oh, this was going to be so beautiful.

The *dude*. What a joke. The "dude" with a "gang." They all knew she was no dude and there was no gang. Just her. It was always just her. And even though not one of them would have ever said it out loud in a million years, Malcolm could at least admit it to himself. He'd been scared of her. They all had. Mal's cousin should have been; he just hadn't known any better. That's why they had all just started staying away from her.

But things were going to change now. No one was going to be scared of that bitch anymore. Now it was her turn to be scared.

EVERY NOW AND THEN GAIA MOORE was convinced that she had stepped into an alternate universe. Some kind of bizarro world where black

Giddy Lovesick Chil[d]

was white and up was down and intensely stupid people were intelligent. Today Starbucks seemed to be that universe. That was the only possible explanation for what she was witnessing.

Chess. A swarm of the absolute dumbest, richest, shallowest party girls the Village School had to offer had all gathered en masse in a corner of Starbucks to watch two boys play *chess*. Actually, from what Gaia could tell, they had really only clumped around one of the boys. Granted, he was attractive enough to warrant a fair amount of attention—tall and slim, with close-cropped flaxen gold hair and the kind of perfectly sculpted features that you usually only see in painted portraits of aristocracy. But still, however attractive this regal boy might be, could that really be enough to make a slew of nitwit FOHs watch an entire chess match as though they were watching a Prada show? It was just a little too strange. And it was making Gaia wish that she had picked anywhere but here to meet Jake after school. But now, unfortunately, she was stuck here until Jake arrived.

She sat on one of the frayed vinyl couches behind a scratched table, a steaming black coffee in front of her, with her legs pulled up against her chest, thumbing through her battered paperback copy of *Crime and Punishment* and pretending she wasn't sneaking a glance, every ninety seconds, out the dirty sunlit windows.

Looking for Jake. Gaia's new favorite pastime.

15

The wall clock said 3:20.

She knew that Jake had math class and that he'd told her he'd come to Starbucks right after he got out. So where *was* he, anyway?

She kept trying to read her book, but she was finding it damn near impossible not to let her eyes drift back up toward the bizarre spectacle in the corner.

For one thing, what the hell was this boy doing playing chess at Starbucks? He must just completely suck. But the longer Gaia watched him play, the more she was forced to give up that theory. He was good. Actually, from what she could see from this distance, he was very good. He was using the king's gambit, for Christ's sake. That wasn't a maneuver for fake chess players. Who the hell was this kid?

Jesus, now I'm doing it.

Gaia suddenly realized that she was apparently no better than the worst of the FOHs. Now she, too, was staring shamelessly at the young chess prince. She shook it off and turned back down to her book. But it wasn't long before her eyes had popped back up and begun to stare.

Of course, there was another reason she probably found this image so compelling. Just how many perfectly sculpted young chess players were there in the world? Gaia had met only one other. And while this boy looked nothing like Sam Moon, how could she not be reminded of the very first time she'd laid eyes on Sam in the park?

Inhumanly good-looking and unexpectedly skilled on the board—it was an unusual combination to say the least. It wasn't that Gaia was attracted to the boy. Those kinds of feelings were now reserved entirely for Jake. But fascinated. . . she couldn't help but be a little fascinated. And neither, it seemed, could any of the rich girls at school.

"Wait," Laura said, leaning down by the boy's ear in an act of shameless flirtation. "If you move your horse there, won't he—?"

The boy silenced Laura by simply placing his finger to his lips. He didn't turn his head or acknowledge her presence in any other way.

"Sorry," Laura whispered earnestly, melting back into the crowd. Gaia couldn't help but smile a little at his total control over the bitchiest of girls and his utter disregard for one of the prettiest of the idiot crew. His priorities were clear. The game first. Doting ninnies later.

"Hey."

And *finally*, there he was—right in front of her. Jake Montone had stepped in front of her view of the chess game, big as life, complete with his gleaming white teeth and smooth olive skin. Gaia looked up at him gratefully as he dropped his book bag and collapsed into the chair opposite her.

"Hey," Gaia said, smiling at him. It was clearly time for her to make a smart-ass comment about him being

17

late. But that was so "old Gaia."

"What—no clever put-down?" Jake said, as if he'd read her mind. He leaned forward and swatted at the book in her hands. "All this Russian literature's messing with your head."

And then they were staring at each other again. Gaia's other new favorite pastime. This was happening all the time now—every time they met, it seemed. A few moments of awkwardly intense staring that continued to leave Gaia with an inexplicable rush of blood to the center of her chest. She always tried to pass it off as more of a staring *contest*, but she had a feeling that Jake could see past her competitive veneer.

"How freakin' weird is this?" he said with a subversive little smile.

"How weird is what?" Gaia asked, feeling an unexpected tinge of insecurity. Was he talking about them? Weird that they'd been making goo-goo eyes at each other? Weird that they were even hanging out like this at all? It *was* weird, wasn't it? It was so out of nowhere. But Gaia had thought it was *good* weird. Didn't Jake think it was good weird?

"This," Jake said, shrugging. "Us. Here. Like this. Weird."

"What's weird about it?" Gaia said, far too defensively. She felt her spine stiffen. "I don't see anything weird about it—we're just. . . I mean, whatever. *You're* weird. . . ."

"Whoa." Jake laughed, squeezing Gaia's hand. "I meant *good* weird."

"Oh." She started to relax again. Maybe she had been burned by this boy-girl thing one too many times. Maybe—

That thought was cut short by the sudden pang of complex emotions jabbing at her heart and pricking her spine. That was always the feeling she got upon spotting Ed Fargo.

Ed and Kai were sitting across from each other at one of the smaller tables in the back of Starbucks, and Gaia's eyes had just met Ed's by accident. It was the kind of moment she and Ed both worked very hard to avoid in school.

That was the standard now between Gaia and Ed. Distance. Distance and avoidance. Gaia still felt like such an extraterrestrial whenever she let herself think about it for too long. How could two people who had been so utterly and completely in love now be going out of their way to avoid anything more than a second's worth of eye contact? She did her best to dump the little pangs of jealousy she was feeling about Ed and Kai, because it was such a ridiculously unfair double standard. Here she was, rushing to Starbucks for another rendezvous with Jake, so what right did she have to be even the least bit resentful of Ed and Kai? None. She had no right whatsoever. Because this was the deal now. This was how things worked. Ed and Kai over there and Gaia and Jake over here. . .

Gaia and Jake. . . She ran the phrase through her head again. *Gaia and Jake*. . . *Is it "Gaia and Jake" now? Is that what we call it?*

Gaia turned back to Jake and began to stare at him again, the rest of the world drifting off into space.

"What?" Jake asked defensively, looking at her again. "What's the problem?"

"No," Gaia assured him. "No, nothing. I wasn't—"

"What was that look?"

"I was just. . ." Gaia found her hands reaching behind her head and fiddling with her hair. She readjusted her ponytail, but it only made the hair fall farther into her face. "Nothing, just. . . It's not a *bad* look," she explained. "I was. . . This is me *happy*, okay?" she announced. She practically slapped Jake in the face with the words, but at least she'd managed to get them out of her mouth. "I mean, this is what I look like when I'm. . . happy."

A grin began to spread across Jake's face. A wide, pearly white, excessively hot, excessively confident grin.

"Stop it," Gaia warned, trying to suppress the embarrassed smile that was about to pop up on her own face. This giddy lovesick child thing was going to give her a goddamn ulcer.

"Stop what?" Jake asked, his smile increasing as he tried to regain eye contact, which was difficult given the fact that Gaia's hand was beginning to involuntarily mask her eyes.

"*Stop it*," she muttered between clenched teeth, "or I swear to God, I will mash your face against this table and that grin will be forever altered." Gaia collected herself and tried to look back in Jake's eyes, but his smile had only grown larger.

"You have no *queen*," the blond chess player taunted his opponent across the room. Now even some adults had come over to watch. The crowd around the table had grown. "You have no rooks, you have no queen. . . you have no chance, my friend."

Jake leaned toward her. "We need to talk," he announced. He locked his eyes so tightly and securely with hers that she didn't even try to avert his glance this time. It was almost like a mild form of hypnosis.

"About what?" Gaia uttered.

"Not now," he said, looking over at the wall clock. "I've got to pick something up for my dad. But we're going to move your stuff over to that boardinghouse later, right?"

"Right. . ."

"So I'll be done in about a half hour. Then we'll walk a little bit before we head uptown. And we'll talk."

"About *what*?" Gaia repeated. But of course some part of her was smarter than that. She could see in his eyes what he wanted to talk about. He wanted to talk

21

about them. He wanted to talk about what was clearly happening between them and what was *going* to happen between them. He wanted to talk about when talking would not be what they spent most of their time doing. He wanted to talk about everything Gaia had been having a delightful time *not* talking about. But exactly how long was she planning to avoid that talk? Old Gaia would have voted for as long as humanly possible, given how ridiculously burned she'd gotten with all this romantic stuff. But new Gaia. . . ? What would new Gaia do?

"Not here," Jake said. "Later. We'll talk. You and me."

Gaia looked deeper in his eyes. "Okay," she heard herself answer.

"Okay," he said. And before he'd even finished that one word, he'd pressed his large hands against the table, leaned his entire torso across, and kissed her. Short, sweet, and deep on the lips. In the middle of Starbucks. With everyone watching.

It was so unexpected. And yet it was so natural. As if it belonged. As if they'd been together for months. And for that one moment Gaia felt like they had been. She felt like everything was right. She felt undeniably normal. For one perfect moment, with Jake's lips pressed to hers, she felt like one of those real girls, complete with real girl tingles down the back of her neck and her real girl hands clasped tightly to her seat. And just as quickly Jake pulled away, backing himself out of Starbucks as he smiled at her.

Then he was out on the street and gone.

A VOICE ECHOED THROUGH ED'S

Star-Crossed Lovers

head. Something about bands that would be playing that night around town. Something else about the movies at the Film Forum. Some part of his brain realized that the voice was Kai's—that she was talking a mile a minute, with her usual unbridled enthusiasm about their potential plans for the evening. But Ed really couldn't hear a word. He couldn't hear Kai, and he couldn't hear the commotion surrounding the nearby table where two boys were playing chess. He couldn't hear much of anything at the moment. All that seemed to matter right now was what he could see.

Gaia and Jake. Kissing. Gaia and Jake kissing across a table in the middle of Starbucks like the happiest teenage lovers in the worst kind of movie.

It was like they were one of those couples whose names had become one word at school: *Are Jake-and-Gaia coming? Hey, did you guys go to Jake-and-Gaia's party last night?* It was making Ed feel unexpectedly ill.

But that really wasn't any of Ed's business anymore, was it? No, that really had nothing to do with Ed in the least.

23

And why the hell do you care? Ed hollered internally as Kai continued to read out options from *The Village Voice. You* don't *care, Ed. You don't give a crap. That's Gaia's life over there. This is your life over here. You and Kai. Making plans. For Christ's sake, you're the one who finally called things off with her, remember?*

Of course he remembered. This was just a freak momentary lapse in sanity, that's all—little moldy leftovers of the kind of jealousy Ed didn't even feel anymore. Gaia deserved to be happy, and so did Ed. And clearly there was no way they could be happy with each other. Gaia's life was just too freaking insane.

Too freaking dangerous.

There was never an ounce of peace in her life, so how could there be an ounce of peace in her relationships? It was impossible. There was always some massive tragedy just around the corner—always some giant horrific detail Gaia was neglecting to mention. A man could not be happy while attached to Gaia Moore. Period.

So what the hell are she and Jake doing in 7th Heaven over there?

"... at the Knitting Factory?"

Ed had missed something. Kai's inflections suggested she'd asked a question.

But what the hell was the question?

"Ed? Hel-*lo*?"

Ed whipped his head back toward Kai and hit her

with a good strong dose of eye contact. "What? Yes," he said blankly. "I mean, *hell*, yes, the Knitting Factory. Definitely."

Kai tilted her head and leaned in closer. Her hair was done up in so many pigtails, she looked like a porcupine. "That's what you want to do?" she asked dubiously.

Ed wished he had any idea what they were talking about. He could think of nothing else but to widen his smile and agree. "Yeah." He nodded emphatically. "I love the Knitting Factory."

"Huh. . . ," Kai uttered, maintaining her perma-smile. "I didn't know you were into `Christian heavy metal. . . .`"

"What?" Ed blurted far too loudly. "Christian heavy—?"

"Where *are* you, Ed?" she groaned. Her smile stayed firm, but Ed could locate true frustration in the corners of her mouth. "You're not listening. Where *are* you today?"

"No, I *am*," Ed insisted. "I'm totally listening." His eyes darted one last time toward Gaia and Jake's table. Jake was backing away toward the plate-glass doors with the most over-the-top star-crossed-lover gleam in his eye. And Gaia was gazing back at him with a look to match. Ed felt his stomach kick, and then he snapped his eyes back toward Kai, wishing very much that he'd resisted the second look. Because she'd caught him looking.

And Ed could see the hurt just barely registering in Kai's eyes.

25

Say something, Ed. Say something fast. Keep the conversation going.

"What about Luna Lounge?" he asked, far too brightly. "Who's playing at Luna tonight?"

Kai didn't respond. Her eyes dropped down momentarily to her lap as her glittering eye shadow reflected the fluorescent lights.

Don't be mad, Ed begged silently. *Please don't be mad. I didn't even mean to look over there. I don't even care what's going on over there.*

"Kai?" He tried to sound as matter-of-fact as possible. "How about Luna?"

Kai took a short breath and then took hold of Ed's hand. It was a most unexpected public display of affection. "You know. . . ," she began slowly, "I have a better idea for tonight."

"Um. . . okay," Ed replied cautiously. He wasn't sure what to make of this particular touch of her hand. But he knew something was different. He knew that in that little moment, Kai had just made some kind of decision.

"How about no music?" Kai seemed to turn on the high beams in her dark brown eyes. "No music, no movie, no X-treme skating event. How about tonight we do something more. . . romantic?"

Ed felt a slight hitch in his throat. Hadn't they sort of been through that approach already? They had tried making things more romantic, but Ed just wasn't quite up to that level yet. Not that Kai wasn't adorably sexy. Not that he didn't love spending all this time with her. Not that they wouldn't probably get extremely romantic sometime very soon, but right now, fooling around with Kai was still kind of awkward.

So how exactly was he supposed to deal with being put on the spot like this?

"Well. . ." *Uh-huh. Good start, Fargo. Smooth.* "I, uh. . . I mean, I think. . ." The longer he stammered, the more he could see Kai's smile beginning to fade ever so slightly.

Don't ruin this, Ed. Kai is awesome. She's hot, she's funny, she's different. She can freaking skate, for God's sake. Do not screw this up. "I think—"

"Checkmate!"

Ed looked over at the chess game. It appeared that the blond boy, whoever he was—Ed had never seen him before—had won. The other boy was sullenly knocking over his own queen. Ed could see only a couple of his pieces remaining on the chessboard.

"Wow—that was so *cool!*" Tannie Deegan squealed reverently. Ed realized that the Friends of Heather had formed an admiring clump behind this young chess genius—and they were all applauding.

And he realized something else as his gaze flicked uncontrollably over to Gaia (and Kai caught him doing it again). Gaia was interested. She was watching.

"Who's next?" The blond boy had started restoring the pieces on the chessboard. "Come on—who's next?

Is there anyone here who can play chess?"

"I'll play! I'll play!" Laura yelled. She was bouncing on her toes with excitement.

The blond chess wizard shook his head condescendingly. "I meant, can anyone here *actually* play chess?"

"Ed?" Kai was asking. She was moving her head around, trying to regain eye contact with him. "What were you saying?"

Gaia was standing up. Ed didn't want to look—he didn't want Kai to see him do it. But it was like he'd lost conscious control of his eyeballs. Gaia was hefting her book bag—and walking over to join the chess players.

"You think what?" Kai was asking. "Ed?"

"Hmmm?" Ed could read Kai's annoyance. "Sorry. I was just—they're playing chess over there," he explained lamely.

"Do you want to go watch?"

"No, I—"

Kai's eyes darted up to meet Ed's. This time she didn't even bother hiding the hurt in her eyes.

"I have to go," Kai said suddenly. She rose out of her chair.

"Wait a minute," Ed complained. He shot up from the table and tried to get some solid eye contact back from Kai. *Make it better, Ed. Make it better fast.* "Wait, I want to talk about tonight," he sort of lied. "I want to make a plan."

"Sure, yeah, anything," Kai said far too bouncily. "I

mean, I'm really up for whatever."

Ed knew she was lying. And he wasn't particularly proud of himself for pretending to believe her. "Okay," he said. "How about bowling?" He smiled. "Tonight? Bowlmor?"

Bowling. Very romantic, Ed.

"Bowling, sure," Kai agreed, staring down at the floor. "I love bowling."

Kai rammed the double doors open with her butt and disappeared without a good-bye or another glance in Ed's direction.

Follow her, asshole, Ed told himself. *Now's the part where you're supposed to follow her.*

Ed sank back into his wooden chair. He picked up his forgotten grande mocha, which was now room temperature.

He should have just gone after Kai and set things straight.

He really should have.

Queen of Toothpaste

"I CAN PLAY," GAIA SAID.

She was standing in front of the wooden table where the blond boy had just

29

soundly defeated the other chess player. The loser had already sullenly shaken hands and left—Gaia saw him over to one side, throwing out his empty paper coffee cup.

The new boy looked up at her. Tannie and Laura and the others stood behind him, glaring at Gaia as if she'd barged into their private room at a country club.

I do believe I'm socializing, Gaia thought dazedly. *Will wonders never cease?*

Standing up, walking over, Gaia had realized that she was behaving strangely. But it felt good; there was no denying it. Jake's kiss was still tingling on her lips as she crossed the room, wondering what possible force of nature could have actually propelled her toward the Friends of Heather and their new boy toy. But strange or not, here she was.

Old Gaia would have buried her nose in her book and fiercely ignored the invitation to play chess. She had come very close to doing just that—it was only a sudden impulse that had made her answer the challenge.

"Can you play a *real* game?" the blond kid demanded. He was frowning sternly at her, as if he was done wasting his time with amateurs.

"Yeah," Gaia said.

Without a word, the blond boy held out his two closed fists.

Gaia pointed at his left hand. He opened it up—it

contained a black pawn.

"Look at that," he remarked bemusedly. "Already losing."

"Do you want to talk," Gaia asked pleasantly, "or do you want to play?"

The boy smiled and made a courteous gesture toward the empty chair facing him.

"The lesson begins," the boy said, advancing the pawn in his king's file. The chess piece clicked against the board, a tiny warrior challenging its enemies.

Gaia didn't bother to speak. She advanced her queen's pawn two ranks.

"Can she do that?" Laura yelled out. "Wait, that's two squares."

"Can't you all go to a shoe store or something?" Gaia asked the Friends of Heather. One move into this game, she was realizing how long it had been since she'd played. She honestly wasn't sure how she would do. "We're concentrating."

Laura glared at Gaia, as if the idea of a girl concentrating on anything besides oatmeal-and-apricot-based facial rinse was unthinkable. "Gaia," she began in her coldest voice, "not like we'd expect you to understand this, but even the most basic social interaction begins with—"

"It's *her*," Megan interrupted. Her perfectly applied mascara fluttered as she stared over Gaia's head at the door to Starbucks. "Oh my *God*—it's her. It's totally her."

Gaia's opponent had made a move. He had brought his queen's bishop out. And she had missed it. It was very annoying.

"It *is* her—oh my *God*," Laura confirmed.

Gaia was staring at the white bishop, but the question distracted her. Who could possibly warrant such a reverent response from the world's most irreverent bitches? Some meaningless Mandy Moore–type celebrity?

Gaia turned her head and followed the FOHs' gaze.

The girl who had just breezed through the glass doors of Starbucks was no celebrity. Gaia was almost sure of it. She just walked like one.

Everything about this girl had the *shine* of a celebrity—her angular cream-colored face, her near floor-length buttery leather coat, the perfect golden highlights of her hair that could only be obtained from the salons on Fifty-seventh Street; even her cat-like tortoiseshell glasses that sat halfway down her elegant nose, attached to a platinum chain that wrapped around her neck. Everything about her was just. . . perfect. Repulsively, hideously, and disgustingly perfect.

"Oh, *Jesus*," Gaia murmured, turning back to the chessboard and making her move.

"What is your problem now?" Megan complained, taking a break from gawking to give Gaia the evil eye. "Gaia, would you like to purchase a clue? Do you even know who that *is*?"

"No, thank God, I don't," Gaia told Megan. *Can't you all just go away?* she thought furiously, watching as Mr. Blond Chess Demon brought out a knight—clearly preparing to castle.

"You will lose this game," Gaia's opponent informed her in his smooth, charming voice, "unless you start paying attention."

"No trash talking," Gaia said, advancing a pawn—not the strongest move she could make, but one that would at least disguise her overall intentions. Meanwhile, she let her eyes drift slightly to the side and watched the girl float up to the counter and order something that surely had a six- or seven-word title—some nonfat, half-soy, double-foam, ten-dollar cup of flavored water.

"That is Elizabeth Rodke," Megan stated. She sounded like she was announcing royalty. "She and her brother have just enrolled at our school."

"Well, three cheers for them," Gaia muttered.

"Okay, I suppose you've never even heard of the Rodke family," Laura said.

"The *who*-key family?"

"Rodke?" Tannie said, staring at Gaia like she was mentally challenged. "As in Rodke and Simon? As in they make just about everything you buy at Duane Reade? Aspirin, soap, shampoo, toothpaste...?"

Gaia's opponent was thoughtfully scratching his

33

chin, grinning privately as he considered his next move. Gaia raised her face and stared directly at the Friends of Heather. Enough, she had decided, was really enough.

"Tannie," Gaia said. "Megan, Laura—let me just make a very small point." They stared back at her, their arms crossed identically, their perfectly waxed eyebrows arrogantly raised. "We"—Gaia indicated herself and the blond boy across from her—"are playing *chess*. That means we're concentrating on an intellectual task. Meanwhile, your queen of toothpaste is over there buying coffee. Once she's *got* her coffee, she'll leave. Now, it seems to me that the smart move for you three would be to *walk away from us* and *go bother her*. Doesn't that seem reasonable?"

Gaia's opponent was smiling at her. Behind him, the FOHs were speechless.

"Whatever," Megan said finally. Then the FOHs mercifully took their leave of Gaia, and, lo and behold, within a matter of seconds they had begun introducing themselves to Elizabeth Rodke.

"Bravo," Gaia's opponent said, staring at the board. With the FOHs gone, it was blessedly quiet. "You've certainly got a way with people."

"Well, how can I kick your ass if neither of us can concentrate?"

"Good point," he agreed while deftly exchanging his king and rook. "And I liked 'queen of toothpaste.'"

"Well, I *hate* that whole status game," Gaia told him. It was funny that she was being so open and honest with someone she didn't even know—but she was liking this blond boy's attitude more and more. "We've got the rest of our lives to be fake and shallow—what's the rush?"

"Ex-*act*-ly." The boy put out his hand. "I'm Chris, by the way."

"Gaia." They shook hands over the chessboard.

Meanwhile, at the counter, the queen had received her royal coffee while Megan, Tannie, and Laura fluttered around her like the loyal subjects they were, trying to make their formal introductions. The whole sight was so sickening. The queen had already begun flashing them her expectedly pearly whites, shaking their hands, and exchanging the most unbearable brand of giggles. She must have recognized instantly that these girls were her "people"—the closest thing the Village School had to an aristocracy.

"Your move," Chris said.

"Right." Gaia tried to tear her eyes away and focus on the chessboard. She wouldn't be missing anything, anyway—the image only grew more grotesque when the queen took a call on her needlessly minuscule cell phone. Now she was weaving her perfect little way through the room, with her soy double-foam nonfat latte in one hand and her little silver cell phone in the other, gabbing away in grandiose fashion as her loyal subjects followed close behind.

She held out her finger to the FOHs with excessive politeness, indicating with another melodramatic grin that she was occupied on the phone. The FOHs kept a respectful distance. Gaia had seen more than enough—she turned back to the game and freed a knight, fortifying her advantage on the board. While she was staring at the pieces, waiting for Chris to make his next move, a shadow fell over the chessboard.

She looked up—and saw that the queen was right there. Standing at their table, making eye contact with Gaia.

Go away, Gaia was screaming internally. *This table is taken. Please, queen of toothpaste, find yourself another goddamn table.*

But the queen didn't budge. She just stood there looking directly into Gaia's eyes, a ludicrously wide smile stretched out across her perfect face. Chris was oblivious—his tanned arm was poised over the chessboard as he prepared to pounce on one of his pieces.

When the queen spoke, however, Gaia became very confused.

"Are they still behind me?" The queen barely moved her mouth to speak. She kept her smile completely intact, but she spoke quietly through her clenched teeth like a ventriloquist. Gaia couldn't tell if she was talking to the phone or to her. But the way she was looking at Gaia, she seemed to be waiting for an answer.

"Are you talking to me?" Gaia finally asked.

"Shhh," she pleaded quietly. "Yes," she uttered through her clenched-teeth grin. "You. I'm talking to you. Are those vultures still behind me?"

Gaia looked behind her and saw the FOHs huddled just a few tables back. They were just standing there, honoring their queen's request for appropriate distance.

"Yeah. They're still there," Gaia reported.

"Oh God." She sighed, maintaining the smile. She turned back toward them and shrugged grandly, pointing to the phone, indicating that she'd probably be on for a while. Then she turned back to Gaia. "Please," she muttered. "Please save me from those girls."

Gaia found a smile creeping across her own face. She was beginning to understand the extent to which she might have misjudged the queen of toothpaste. "What should I do?" Gaia asked.

"Can I just sit down at this table for a minute and finish my fake phone call? I won't disturb your game; I promise."

"Well—sure."

"Thank you." Rolling her eyes with relief, the queen dropped down in the chair next to Gaia and indicated once more to the FOHs that her call was going to be a while. She kept the phone glued to her ear and continued to speak into it. "Uh-huh. . . uh-huh. . . *right*. . ." She snuck another look at Gaia. "Are they gone yet?"

37

Gaia looked back and saw Megan, Laura, and Tannie finally give up on the wait. They headed for the door. "They're leaving."

The queen breathed a sigh of relief, slumping in her chair.

Finally she turned to Gaia. "Thank you *so* much," she told Gaia. "I thought there was no escape. I'm Liz, by the way."

"*Got* you," Chris blurted. He grabbed his knight and took Gaia's queen's pawn. "I'll forgive you for being distracted. Hey, sis."

"Hey, Chris," the queen of toothpaste said, closing her cell phone and dropping it on the table. "So we made it through our first day, huh?"

"Barely," Chris agreed. "Gaia, this is my sister, Liz Rodke. Liz, this is Gaia."

Sister—?

Gaia could feel her face flushing. The FOHs had mentioned that the queen had a brother. They'd apparently had no idea that he was sitting right here, playing chess with Gaia. And Gaia had called her—

"You're the queen of toothpaste, by the way," Chris said pleasantly.

"Queen of—" Liz Rodke was laughing. "Wait, that's hilarious."

"I thought so, too," Chris said. Gaia's face was burning. She had no idea what to say."

"I—I am so *sorry*," Gaia stammered. "I didn't mean—"

Liz touched Gaia's arm reassuringly. "Please don't worry about it. I'm the one who pays the price of being known. Chris is anti–society page. I get so jealous."

"So you've both started at the Village School?" Gaia asked, still so flustered, she'd lost sight of her strategy.

"Yeah, where apparently you're the queen," Liz said.

"So we've come to the right place if we want to get acquainted," Chris went on.

I'm the queen of the school? Gaia thought wildly. *That's the most ridiculous thing I've ever heard.*

Of course, the Rodkes had just arrived at the Village School. It wasn't their fault—they would soon find out how ridiculous that premise was.

"But I'm not—" Gaia began.

"This girl has been dominating Starbucks since she got here," Chris insisted, looking up from the chessboard. "She's got a very pretty boyfriend whom she kissed good-bye about five minutes ago, and everyone in the room watched. Especially that equally lovely boy in the back of the room."

He means Ed, Gaia realized. *He hasn't missed a thing.*

"And those three badly dressed cows are *desperately* jealous of her," Chris went on. "I'm pretty jealous myself, with all the male attention she's getting."

"Gaia, do those girls represent the majority of the student body?" Liz was smiling a real smile this time— it was easy to see the difference. And her name was

Liz. Not Queen Elizabeth. Not the queen of toothpaste. Just Liz. "Because that would be bad."

"No, I think you've seen the worst of it right there," Gaia said. "You didn't have to be so nice to them."

"Yes, I did. I've learned that the hard way. If I gave those girls an ounce of attitude, then I'd get a permanent rep at this school in two seconds: *rich bitch*. Boom."

Gaia felt instantly guilty. Liz had Gaia's first impression of her totally pegged. And it wasn't fair. She didn't want to be judged for her gray sweatshirt. Why should Liz be judged for her leather coat?

"But you *are* a rich bitch, sis," Chris said, while staring at the chessboard. Liz thwacked him on the shoulder without looking.

"Besides," Liz went on. "Nice is just easier. You know what I mean?"

"I guess," Gaia said dubiously. "Where are you from? I'm sorry—I suck at small talk."

"No, that's *good*," Liz assured her. "Small talk takes up half of my life. We much prefer 'actual' talk. We're always making speeches; you can't shut us up. It's awful."

"Who's 'we'?"

"My whole family," Liz replied, taking a sip from her coffee. "My father and mother, me—even dimwit here."

"I make speeches, I play chess," Chris agreed readily, "and I'm smart enough to befriend the school's most popular girl since it's the easiest way to meet the cutest boys."

"But I'm not—"

Gaia stopped, looking down at the table and at the white and black queens facing each other across the chessboard.

I'm not popular.

But Liz wasn't what she seemed, either, was she? Not to Gaia or to the FOHs. And neither was Chris—she hadn't guessed that he was gay until he'd made it clear.

What's real? What's a pose? What are people you haven't met yet like? How can you tell?

Life as new Gaia was getting interesting.

And for just
one moment
Gaia could
see it in
Jake's eyes: **the**
actual **power**
terror. Real
live child-
like terror.

Dear Gaia,

You and I have so much catching up to do. Years' and years' worth. So I thought I might try writing you letters. For me as much as for you, I suppose. Just to try and connect with you as much and as often as possible. I need that.

I'm writing for two reasons. The first is to let you know just how sorry I am for everything that's happened. It isn't easy for me to face the truth of what I was and what I've done over the years— to you, to your father, to your poor mother, and to so many innocent people. The only chance I have of finding any kind of peace is if I try to keep making amends and try to devote myself to being the best person I can be and the best uncle I can be to you. When I look in the mirror, I want to see plain Oliver Moore and not that monster, Loki, and all the terrible things he's done. That's only possible if I make amends with the people I've hurt. And that means Tom and you, Gaia.

Here's the second reason I'm writing, Gaia. I want you to know that you can depend on me. You're a very brave and very intelligent young woman, and you certainly don't need an old uncle's help to live your life. You've shown over and over again that you're more than capable of holding your own. But if there's anything you need, ever, at any time—especially with Tom out of New York—please don't hesitate to let me know, and I'll take care of it. It would be an honor.

Like you, I'm sure, I'm doing my best to resume a normal life and put all the events of the past behind me. I've moved into this new apartment on Broome Street. It's not that far from your school—just a short walk across town. I'd love it if you came by to see it. You're welcome anytime, along with Jake or any of your friends you want to bring, whenever you just want to get away from everything and relax.

It's strange, as a middle-aged
man, to try to resume a life that
I never really led to begin with.
But it feels good to be doing the
right thing and to be on the right
side again. I don't know how I
ever could have gotten so lost and
so turned around, as I was for all
those years. It seems like just
yesterday that I was wrestling
with your father when we were kids
or dropping by that rat's nest of
an apartment he had up by
Columbia. Those memories are so
vivid, it's hard to believe that
I've been robbed of all the time—
time I could have been spending
with you or your father or even
with Katia. I'd give anything to
go back and do it over, but of
course that's impossible.

Nikolai is dead already—I know
that. There's no way to kill him
again for what he did to me, to all
of us. And of course Yuri is finally
out of our lives. I find it difficult to think about that—that monster, that abomination—without being
overcome with rage. All the things

he took from us, from all of us;
things we can never get back. . . .
It's probably best for me not to
think about that.

But I can't help it. In the
end, the blame goes all the way
around, doesn't it? We all played
our parts in the big game, and we
each made our mistakes. In the
end, it was a game about being
smart, wasn't it? About having
the willpower and the intelligence to control events by con-
trolling the people around you.
Gaia, if you had joined my side,
we could have taken control of
all of it. I'm sure you realize
that. The smartest and bravest
people end up in charge, and who
can argue with that? It was stupidity, plain human stupidity
that caused all the sadness and
loss in our lives. Tom's awful
stupidity first, the way he stole
Katia away from me. Then
Rodriguez at the CIA, but let's
face facts, Gaia, when have they
ever been smart about anything?
It makes me so angry. And anger

helps me see the truth. *And the real truth is that the only way to get what you want in this world is to be smart enough and brave enough to force things your way. You can't have the life you want if you're afraid of your own power—you have to* take control *of*

OLIVER STOPPED WRITING.

He raised his head and looked around. He felt dizzy. For a moment he wasn't sure where he was.

Violent Tendencies

But of course he knew exactly where he was. The smell of coffee and the ticking clock told him: he was at his own kitchen counter in the middle of his new loft. Behind him, the empty living room reflected the bright afternoon sunshine from the skylights high in the wall. There was no sound but the ticking of the antique clock over the refrigerator and the murmur of Manhattan traffic outside.

Oliver looked down at the letter he'd been writing. He massaged his hand, which was aching and throbbing. It was easy to see why: the ballpoint writing, which looked so mild and neat at the top of the letter, got darker and more violent as it went down the page. The last paragraph was written in thick block letters, gouged deeply into the lined paper. Oliver saw that he'd actually torn the paper as he wrote.

He put the pen down on the counter and took a sip of coffee. It soothed him. He took a deep breath, looking over the letter, and then, in one fast move, he ripped the page from the pad and savagely crumpled it up. He had to crumple the next page, too, since the savage writing had gone through the paper.

A loud buzzer went off. Oliver jumped, spilling the coffee onto the stone counter.

What the hell?

It was the door buzzer, Oliver realized. Somebody was here to see him. He had never heard the sound before. In the short time he'd lived at this new Broome Street loft, nobody had ever come to visit. He had no idea who it could be.

Gaia?

That would be nice, Oliver thought as he crossed the wide floor toward the big industrial front door. It would be nice if Gaia dropped by. *Speak of the devil,* he would say, smiling and hugging her. *I was just writing to you.*

Then he would offer her coffee, and they would sit on his new Bauhaus sofas and talk, and for a little while he could put the past behind him.

His footsteps clattered loudly in the vast, empty loft. He remembered the landlady who had shown him the place, pointing out the skylights and the stone kitchen counter and the metal door and all the other beautiful details. The middle-aged realtor had smiled at Oliver flirtatiously as she showed him around, explaining how he could cook for twenty in the huge kitchen when he gave a dinner party. He didn't tell her that he never gave dinner parties because he didn't have any friends. *I may look like a forty-year-old man about town,* he could have told her, *but you don't know the truth.*

"Who is it?" Oliver called out.

"Mr. Moore?"

It was a male voice. Muffled by the thick metal door but clearly a young man's. Oliver didn't recognize the voice at all.

"Yes?"

"Mr. Moore, this is Agent Rowan with Central Intelligence. I'd like to talk to you for a few minutes, if that's all right."

Oliver cringed.

Agent Rowan?

He didn't know any Agent Rowan. In all the hours the CIA had spent interrogating him, pumping him for every piece of information about his activities in the Organization, tape recording every word he'd said, he hadn't met an Agent Rowan.

But I can't say that, Oliver thought. Standing there with his thumb on the intercom button, with his coffee getting cold on the counter behind him, Oliver realized that he had to let the man in. Because the last thing he could afford to do was look suspicious or like he had anything to hide. With his history, his background, the things he'd done, it was a miracle he wasn't in a Guantanamo Bay prison. He was lucky to be alive, let alone relaxing in an expensive New York loft.

Rowan was a new agent; that was all. They hadn't met. Fine. Everything was going to be *fine*.

Relax. Act natural. Cooperate. Be good, Ollie.

Oliver pulled the door open.

Rowan wasn't alone. There was another man with him. They both wore drab suits and ties like CIA, but Oliver still didn't recognize them.

"Mr. Moore? I'm Jim Rowan," the taller, younger agent said. He gestured at the other man. "This is Agent Morrow."

Ask to see their badges. Ask for a warrant.

But he couldn't do any of that. He had to appear as cooperative as possible. He had to get on with this.

"Come in." Oliver smiled, stepping back and holding the door for them. "Would you like some coffee?"

"No, thank you," Rowan said briskly. Morrow followed him into the room.

"What can I do for you?" Oliver said warmly. He led them into the loft, toward where he'd been sitting.

"Well, we're still trying to wrap up some loose ends, Mr. Moore," Rowan explained, pulling a small voice recorder from his shirt pocket. "We just have a few more questions for you, all right?"

Oliver could feel his pulse speeding up, but he kept himself in check. "All right." He sat down, aiming to look as neutral as possible. The sooner they got through this, the sooner they would leave.

"Good." Rowan spoke deliberately into the machine. "Mr. Moore, what can you tell us about a Doctor Glenn?"

Oliver's mouth went dry. He stood up and walked to the sink to pour himself a glass of water. "Dr.

Glenn? Well. . . didn't we cover Dr. Glenn in the Agency interrogation already?"

Oliver could see a hint of annoyance in Rowan's eyes. "Of course," Rowan said. "Yes, we did. . . but. . . we'd like to go over it once more, all right? Dr. Glenn. We've recovered the majority of his files, but there's still a great deal missing. Blood work on Gaia Moore, DNA coding tests on Ms. Moore, some documentation on Glenn's serum. What can you tell us about that serum and those missing files? Where would we locate those missing test results?"

Oliver had trouble paying attention to anything Rowan had said after the word *serum*. It was a word he would have been more than happy never to hear again. That fearless serum had been among the most heinous of Loki's twisted endeavors, and the last thing Oliver wanted to do was focus on it or the lives it had ruined.

Talking about the serum was only going to bring out the worst in him.

And he was trying very hard to present his best.

"Look, I'm. . . I'm so sorry," Oliver said, working harder to maintain the smile. "But I really have told the Agency everything I know about that serum and Dr. Glenn and everything else that. . . Loki did. . . and so I really think you'd be best off just going back and checking the Agency transcripts for—"

"Mr. Moore, we've been *through* the transcripts," Rowan complained. "We would just like you to answer some of the questions again. For our records. Why don't you just answer the questions and we'll be done here much sooner, all right?"

Oliver locked his eyes with Rowan's. He didn't care for his tone at all, but he was trying to stay in control. And control seemed to be something that was increasingly difficult for Oliver lately, particularly when Loki's actions were being discussed.

Stay calm. Stay calm at all costs. Do whatever you have to do.

"Look, Agent Rowan." Oliver smiled through clenched teeth. "Maybe we could just... reschedule this interview for a little later. I do have some appointments I should really—"

"Mr. Moore, this isn't a *social* visit. We don't reschedule at your convenience." Rowan challenged Oliver with his eyes. And Oliver didn't like it. He didn't like it one bit. He felt his hand forming a fist and quickly focused all his energy on stretching the fingers apart. He turned to Agent Morrow and smiled.

"Agent Morrow, please," Oliver said sweetly. "You can understand how difficult for me this is, can't you? Don't you think you might be able to speak with your partner here about relaxing his attitude—?"

"*Moore*," Rowan snapped. He shot up out of his chair and stepped much closer to Oliver's face. "Are we having a communication problem here, Moore? I think we're having a communication problem. Because I just need you to answer the *questions*. That's it. That is all.

The equation could not be simpler. You tell us where the missing files on Gaia are, and we *leave*. Do you understand? *Simple*. Cut-and-dried. Where are those files?" Rowan thrust his hand forward and stuck his digital recorder back into Oliver's face.

Suddenly Oliver found himself reexamining Rowan's deeply frustrated eyes. And his slightly wrinkled suit. And his slightly loosened tie.

Because Oliver Moore had been with the CIA for many years in another life. And "Agent" Rowan had just broken Agency protocol with almost every word he'd said. "Agent" Rowan had suddenly seemed much less like an agent and much more like a man who was hungry for information. Information that the CIA should have given him already—if he *was* in fact with the Agency. . . .

"I'm sorry—who are you again?" Oliver uttered suspiciously. He faced down "Agent" Rowan as he pushed the recorder out of his face.

There was the slightest delay in Rowan's reply. "*Excuse* me?" he asked indignantly.

"I said, *who are you*?" Oliver repeated, his eyes beginning to narrow. "If you have a badge, I'd like to see it. Because I'll tell you one thing: You're not CIA." Now he wasn't working quite so hard to keep his fist from clenching. In fact, he wasn't working at all.

Rowan glanced back to Morrow momentarily, who seemed unsure how to react. "Mr. Moore. . . I'm not sure what exactly you are trying to pull here, but I suggest you stop it right now. We really don't want to have to—"

"To *what*?" Oliver spat. "To take me down to headquarters? Where *are* headquarters, 'Agent' Rowan? Do you know? Can you tell me?"

"Mr. Moore, I think you're acting a bit unstable here."

"Do you?"

"Yes, I do."

"Then why don't you take me in?" Oliver presented his wrists to Rowan. "I suggest you take me in right now, *Agent* Rowan, before I turn any more unstable."

Rowan began to back away slowly from Oliver. "Mr. Moore, I am warning you. Stay calm. I believe you're becoming paranoid right now, and it is important that you remain calm. Peter. . ." Rowan was signaling for Morrow to get involved, but Morrow didn't seem any more confident about what to do, either.

"Who are you working for?" Oliver demanded. "Who the *hell* are you working for? Who *are* you?" Suddenly Oliver had grabbed hold of Rowan's shirt and tugged him much closer. Hs fist was clenched so tightly now, he could feel his own fingernails digging into the skin of his palm. "What do you want from *Gaia*? I swear, if you go anywhere *near* her, if you touch a hair on her *head*, I will—"

"All right, *enough*!" Rowan shouted. "That's *enough*."

Oliver felt something jab at his stomach, and he realized that Rowan had pulled his gun.

"All right, step *back*," Rowan ordered. "Get your hand off of me, Moore, and take two steps back. *Now*."

"Why don't you just take me in?" Oliver dared the obvious phony. "What are you waiting for?"

"You need psychiatric assistance, Mr. Moore. We'll be filing a report on this incident, *believe* me. Paranoid, unstable, violent tendencies—it's all going into my report." Rowan and Morrow backed quickly toward the door.

"I'll find out who you are," Loki shouted. "Who you *really* are, I mean. You can count on it. You have no idea who you're dealing with here! *No* idea!"

Rowan slammed the door behind him, and Oliver could hear the two phonies scuffling for the stairs. He ran and hoisted the door open again, shouting down the stairwell at them. "Stay away from Gaia Moore!" he hollered. "I am warning you!"

Oliver slammed the door behind him. Leaning against the door, he realized he was sweating like mad. His heart was pounding, and there was a slight trembling in his hands.

Who were they? What just happened?

Looking over at the kitchen counter, Oliver saw the crumpled note he'd written to Gaia.

Anger helps me see the truth, he'd said.

Oliver nodded. He was angry. And there was something else, too.

He was frightened. Frightened for Gaia.

FIELD REPORT: INTERVIEW WITH SUBJECT A-2-A

Rowan, J., and Morrow, P., reporting

Interview was conducted at 11:50 A.M. EST at subject's address. The subject, Oliver Moore, aka Loki (see attached file 45071-a), gave ambiguous answers to several questions (concerning the serum we have code-named BLUEBELL) before terminating the interview and physically assaulting the interviewers. Attempts to convince the subject to resume the discussion failed.

Throughout, the subject showed signs of instability, anger, and nervousness, which are clearly associated with the "Loki" personality. This instability was expressed as paranoid delusion: Mr. Moore referred both to his CIA training and to the more lethal techniques he had developed in his role in the Organization.

The information provided by the subject was inconclusive, and given Moore's refusal to cooperate further, the investigation must proceed using different methods.

Arrangements are being made for the next interview to be conducted within days, allowing for travel time (to upstate New York) and other factors. A subsequent field report will be submitted thereafter through the usual channels.

END

THIS WASN'T JAKE. NOTHING ABOUT

this was Jake. Jake didn't wait. Jake
didn't hesitate. Jake wasn't patient.
If there was something he wanted,
he set his sights, and he locked on
target, and he went for it.

Pathetic Hesitancy

Be a man. That was the point. It
was a stupid, ancient, macho
cliché, fine, but that didn't make the sentiment any
less true, and it didn't mean they weren't words to live
by. They were in fact words Jake generally lived by.
And they had done him nothing but good for the first
eighteen years of his life. So why should this be any
different? Why should tonight be any different?

But it was different. It was different because it was
Gaia. And that meant a few things. It meant that what
was happening between them was a little more awkward than it should have been—than it ever had been
for him before. It meant that it was serious because
Gaia was serious: she didn't titter and squeal and chase
after boys and parties like the majority of the girls he'd
spent his time with. And most of all, it meant that it
was complicated. Gaia was complicated. Her life was
way more than complicated. Jake might consider himself a pretty simple guy, but nothing was simple when
it came to this girl. He knew that. He understood that.

But still, it was time. It was time to make his point.
It was time to get the words out. It was time to tell her

that he didn't want to wonder anymore. He didn't want to wonder exactly where they stood or where they were going. He wanted the whole thing—the entire package. Jake and Gaia. Boyfriend and girl-friend. Completely committed and together. Fighting, walking, eating, sleeping. Together.

And sex. Yes, he wanted that. He wanted that very badly. But the point here—the *real* point here... was love.

Jake was in love with her. And he simply needed to know that she was in love with him. Which he was very much starting to believe she was.

Or maybe she wasn't? She was so goddamn awkward, serious, and complicated, he still honestly wasn't sure. "This is my boyfriend, Jake." Those were the simple words he wanted to hear coming out of Gaia's mouth. But did she want it or not? The only way to know was to ask. To ask her point-blank.

So why had he spent the last who-knows-how-many hours with her walking and hanging out all over the Village, doing everything but? They'd talked about every other conceivable topic. They'd eaten hot dogs from Gray's and fake ice cream. She had rested in his lap on park benches and given him light kisses on the stoops of brownstones. She'd held his hand almost the entire time they'd walked, which, from what Jake understood, was a pretty un-Gaia-like thing to do. Of course, they were supposed to be head-ing up to her Seventy-second Street apartment to pack up all her things and move her down to that boarding-house, but neither one of them had really wanted to get to that. It seemed like they'd both just wanted the evening to go on like this for as long as humanly possible, without ever calling it a night.

But he still hadn't asked her. He *still* hadn't found the right moment to lay it on the line. And it was only getting darker and darker. And he was only starting to feel more and more like a chicken. Less and less like a man.

And as it got on past eight, they had found themselves coming nearly full circle as they strolled onto the darkened pavement of Washington Square Park. Which was fine with Jake. Because it somehow seemed like the most appropriate place to ask. It was her place, Jake knew that. It sort of represented her somehow. Urban and beautiful. Gorgeously light when it was light and incredibly dark when it was dark. And maybe now Washington Square Park could be the place Jake and Gaia remembered as the exact spot where they officially started going out.

Jake finally shook off his `pathetic hesitancy` and grabbed hold of Gaia's arms under a huge overhanging tree, planting her still on the ground so he could look straight into her eyes and cut the crap.

"Gaia."

"Jesus, what?" Gaia's eyes widened with surprise at the force of Jake's hands around her arms. Jake loosened his grip a bit. But not much. This was too important.

"Gaia, listen," he said quietly. "I don't know what's wrong with me here. I'm avoiding my ass off. So just listen."

"Jake—"

"No, listen." The wind had kicked up through the park, carrying that uniquely New York sound that combined distant traffic and a far-off industrial whir with the rustling leaves of the trees. The huge expanse of white noise surrounding them only made their voices seem closer.

"You know," Jake said, "every day I'm zoning out completely through all my morning classes, just staring at the clock. I burn freaking holes in that thing, trying to force the hands to hit twelve so I can break for that stupid cafeteria and find you."

"I know," she said, puffing out an embarrassed little laugh. "Me too. It's sick, isn't it?"

"No, it's not sick. There's nothing sick about it. The same way there's nothing sick about the way I want to find you after school. And stay with you for the rest of the day. And stay with you for the rest of the night. It's not sick, Gaia, it's just—it's just. . . what we should be. I mean really be. Officially. You know what I mean?"

Jake searched Gaia's eyes for clues. But the deeper he searched, the less he could understand. And the longer she stayed silent, the more he was starting to feel like the world's biggest asshole.

NOW'S THE PART WHERE YOU'RE SUP-posed to talk. Isn't that obvious?

Every additional word in Gaia's head was only making her pathetic silence last longer.

Invincible

And so the silence went longer and longer as an endless stream of words piled up in her head.

So much of her wanted to break the goddamn old-Gaia spell. She knew what Jake wanted. She knew what he was asking for. She'd known it all day. He wanted the whole thing. The real thing. The full commitment. And so much of her wanted it, too. So much of her wanted this to be a huge part of her new beginning. It started with her family, but getting things right with Jake was just as important. She didn't just want to give over fully to Jake; she *needed* to. She needed to prove to herself that she could do it.

Old Gaia couldn't. She'd proved that with Sam. She'd proved it with Ed. Old Gaia couldn't make it work. Not with her life in a continuous shambles. Not with sick, twisted assholes chasing her down and ripping her heart out all the time. But new Gaia. . . new Gaia didn't have all that crap to contend with anymore. At least, she wasn't supposed to. . . .

But God help her, she still couldn't shake it. She couldn't shake off all the times she'd been burned before—all the innocent people she'd hurt. She couldn't drag another boy in. Even if the danger seemed miles away—even if it *seemed* like it was never coming back—she couldn't trust it. She couldn't bring another boy into the middle of that danger ever again.

Except. . . in Jake's case. . . maybe she could?

Jake could handle himself. If that danger ever presented itself again, they could help each other. They could *protect* each other.

And what if the danger never did resurface? What if the danger was truly over? She could go on for years like this, never letting anyone into her life, only to find years later that she'd lived her whole life alone for no good reason.

No. She had to take the leap. She had to. She had to believe that the danger was gone. If she couldn't take that leap, then there was no way she could truly start her life as new Gaia. And if she couldn't be new Gaia, then there was really no point in anything anymore. New Gaia was the entire and only point now.

She had to tell Jake that she was ready. Whether she was or not. She had to tell him that she was ready to go there. . . .

"Oh, that is *so her*, man. That is *so* the very same *bitch*!"

The repellent voice had blared out from the bushes just across the pavement. Gaia dropped her eyes from Jake's and scanned the bushes, trying to target the origin of the voice.

No, no. Not now. This has to be a joke. Someone is

*trying to play a practical joke on me here, and they just
don't know that they've chosen a very, very bad time.*

"Oh, man, what the hell was that?" Jake growled,
pounding his fist back against the tree. He was clearly
just as frustrated as Gaia was with this asshole's tim-
ing. If the dude wanted to pick a fight *any* other night,
any other time, that would have been just fine by Gaia.
`One more god-awful street spat in the
park for old times' sake.` If it had to be, it
had to be. But not *now*. Not at this particular moment.

"Gaiaaaa," another voice called out. "Is that Gaiaaaa?"
Then he howled out the most disturbing and pathetic
cackle.

*Great. Now there are two of them. That's just exactly
what I need right now.*

"Let's just take 'em," Jake said, moving in front of
Gaia to protect her. "We deal with them, and then we
get back to our conversation."

"No, Jake, let's just go," Gaia complained, pulling
him back behind her. "We don't need anymore of
this—"

"Let's *slice* and *dice!*" another voice howled out.

And before Gaia and Jake could even move, they
suddenly found themselves in the middle of the fastest
ambush she had seen in quite some time.

There were at least six of them. No, seven. Then
eight. Skinheads, of course. The world's most ignorant
brotherhood. With their offensive swastika T-shirts,

and their ten thousand piercings all chained together, and their stupid hard-core combat boots, and their `phallic-substitute Leatherman knives.` All the same old crap.

Only something was different. Something was very different. In their eyes. In the expressions on their faces. Even their voices...

"You're going to eat this knife," one of them bellowed, creeping quickly toward her. "You're going to swallow the entire thing, and you're going to bleed." He seemed to be the leader. He had no shirt on, and his body was covered in white-power tattoos. A big silver swastika earring was dangling from his left ear. His black eyes were stretched twice as wide as they should have been, darting from side to side with `the manic speed of an insect.` He was practically foaming at the mouth.

They all had that look. The same wide vibrating eyes. The veins bulging out from their necks like they were about to burst. What was this? What the hell was wrong with them?

Gaia and Jake both began to crouch into a fighting stance.

"Do you have any idea how long I've been *waiting* for this?" the leader said as his boys moved closer and closer from all sides like starving wolves. The words were pouring out of his mouth like vomit, one after the other, faster and faster. "Do you know how *long* we've all been hiding like freaking *girls* from the big bad Gaia *bitch*?"

Gaia could practically see his heart pounding, trying to rip its way right out of his chest. His head was shaking harder and harder with every word. What the hell was he on?

"What's wrong with you?" Gaia uttered. "What's wrong with all of—?"

"We were goddamn cowards!" he shouted. "We were all cowards! We didn't have the *power.*"

They all hollered their agreement as their mouths spread into wide, manic grins.

"The power of *God*!" one of them shouted.

"Hell, yes! That is the power of *God*, bitch. The power to reach down your throat, tear your freaking heart out, and *eat* it. And tonight's the night. Tonight is dead Gaia night! This is for my cousin."

And then he lunged. He lunged hard and fast. Faster than she'd expected. Faster than either one of them had expected.

"Jake!" Gaia hollered, dropping and rolling to her right.

Jake whipped his body back against the tree, just barely dodging the full-force swipe of the blade.

"Bye-bye!" The leader had started to giggle as he took another full swing at Jake with wide-eyed abandon. "Bye-bye! Bye-bye! Bye-bye!" Jake leapt for the bushes and rolled to safety, but he was met with a stiff black combat boot to the head.

And then they were all shouting it—choruses of gleeful "bye-byes" as they mercilessly stormed Gaia and Jake.

Gaia shut out every sound. Her eyes took over as her body locked into a purely unconscious focus. Knife by knife, face by face, she began picking her targets and her order of moves. And then she sprang into action. Literally.

Her body floated over the grass as her leg snapped out at the first knife, ripping it from one of the psycho's hands. She landed directly in front of him, cramming her knee into his groin as he doubled over and then shooting her foot forward straight at his chin, sending his entire torso back like a rag doll.

Jake leapt off the ground and grabbed one of their wrists, twisting the skinhead's entire arm back and then tossing him overhead. His chain-covered body careened forward headfirst into the tree with a loud, jangling thud.

"Gaia, behind you!" Jake warned.

Before she'd even turned her head, she snapped her elbow behind her, cracking the nose of whoever it was standing there. Then she reached back, felt for his center, and flipped him directly onto his pathetic bony ass. He let out a loud sound as he writhed on the ground.

But it wasn't the sound of pain....

It was the sound of laughter. His writhing body had given in to fits of laughter. And then, quite suddenly, he pounced back up off the ground and came at Gaia again. Even harder and faster this time.

She had to move double time to deal with his insanely adrenalized speed. And she had to hit harder to take him out. She leapt up for a huge sweeping roundhouse kick to the face. His face snapped to the right as blood gushed from his mouth, but then he came at her *again*. She needed a second roundhouse kick at double the strength to send his entire body three feet back and finally knock him out.

This wasn't right. This was all wrong. Skinheads were easy. Skinheads were the bottom of the barrel as far as fighting was concerned. The trained martial artists were supposed to be the problem, and the Navy SEALs and those SWAT-like sons of bitches in black. These kids were street trash. Gaia had dumped the likes of them into trash cans without breaking a sweat. But these sons of bitches had changed. They were the same assholes she'd seen around the park a hundred times before, but they *weren't* the same. It wasn't that they were skilled in any way. They just... wouldn't stop.

"You idiot!" the leader howled at Jake. "You idiot!" He laughed. "You *can't* freaking scare me! I don't *bleed* anymore. Nothing *hurts*. I don't bleed. *You* bleed." He drove his knife at Jake's chest—straight for the center of his chest with every intention of gutting him. And for just one moment Gaia could see it in Jake's eyes: actual terror. `Real live childlike terror.`

"Jake!"

The knife ripped through Jake's T-shirt and pierced his skin.

But Gaia reached out in time. She swung her hand around the leader's neck and ripped him backward right off his feet as they went tumbling to the ground. His six-foot frame nearly crushed her to the ground as he lay on top of her on his back.

"Drop it!" Gaia shouted, pulling tighter and tighter around his neck as his breaths became fewer and farther between. He was bucking and kicking his entire body, trying to break free from Gaia's choke hold. His hand grasped his knife even tighter as he tried to lunge behind him for any part of Gaia's body over and over again. He was lunging so wildly that he actually sliced open his own arm.

But it made no difference. Blood was pouring from his left arm and he hadn't made a sound. Not even the least indication of pain. He only swung back harder and harder. "I don't bleed," he choked out between strangled giggles. "I'm invincible, *bitch*. You can't touch me. . . ."

Jake had obviously been enraged by his near-death experience. He went off on the bastards in a frenzy, disarming their cackling attacks with a kick and then snapping some bones when he had to. Whatever it took to take these mindless psycho-skinheads out.

But Gaia had to stay focused on this one lunatic—the boy who seemed totally unaware that not only *did* he bleed, but that he *was* in fact bleeding profusely from his own self-inflicted wound. "I... said... *drop it*," Gaia uttered.

She finally applied enough pressure to his windpipe that he passed out. His body went completely limp on top of hers, and she hurled him off of her, leaping back onto her feet in one smooth motion. She snatched up his knife and ran for the last psycho still standing.

She waved the knife right in his face. "It's over!" she warned him. "Unless you want to end up in pieces, I suggest you get the hell out of here!"

But he only laughed harder, like he'd just shared the most hysterical joke with himself. "Go ahead," he chortled. "Cut me! Try to cut me!" He jumped up and down in place like a hyperactive child. "I want you to. I *dare* you to. It's not going to hurt. It's not." And then his laughs began to give way to a terrible coughing fit. "Oh Jesus," he spat out between coughs. "Oh God, I love it. Thank you, God. . . I love it." And then he dropped down to his knees and clasped his hands over his eyes. "Oh God." He coughed again. "My head. My freaking head."

Slowly Gaia let the knife drop to the ground as she watched this pathetic sight. The boy gripped his head tighter and tighter, and then finally he collapsed, falling back into the grass with a light thud.

Gaia stared down at his body with utter puzzlement. She knelt down next to him and checked for a pulse. He was still breathing. He was just gone for the night.

She felt a hand come down on her shoulder. But she instantly knew that it was Jake's. This particular nightmare was finally over.

"Are you okay?" he asked.

"I'm fine," she said, trying to catch her breath. "It's them I want to know about. What the hell happened to them?" She scanned the unconscious bodies strewn about her and tried to make sense of the strangest attack she'd ever experienced.

"Can you stand up?"

"Of course," Gaia said. She made a move to stand up, and then all of Washington Square Park began to spin in huge swooping circles. "Or actually, Jake, will you help get me back uptown?"

"Of course," Jake said, kneeling down next to her and checking the bruises on her face.

"Good. Because I think I'm going to. . ."

The last thing she felt was Jake's arms catching her before she hit the ground.

GOD, WHAT IS THIS, "LOVERS' NIGHT"
or something?

Ed's annoyance level was spiking as he scanned the line of bowling lanes at Bowlmor. Couple after couple after couple. All of them slapping fives and swigging from their beers and then, of course, kissing. A kiss for every strike, every spare, every gutter ball; it didn't seem to matter. Madonna's "Like a Virgin" was blaring through the speakers, and somehow Bowlmor had been transformed into some sort of fifties-style make-out palace. And it just kept inducing the same damn flashback over and over again in Ed's head.

Jake and Gaia. Jake and Gaia smiling. Jake and Gaia gleaming with the light of *teenage love in the afternoon.*

Jake and Gaia kissing. Over and over.

It was only in the last few minutes that Ed had begun to understand why this nagging image refused to leave his head—why it was making him so excessively annoyed. The reason wasn't jealousy. The reason was this:

If there was such a thing as an alternate universe—some reality that existed somewhere else in time and space—and if Ed and Gaia just *happened* to be existing in that alternate universe somewhere. . . then it should have been *them* kissing across that table in Starbucks. Not that Ed wanted that now, but back *then. . .* back when they'd been together, back in that alternate universe, a simple moment like that was all he had wanted.

A moment of normalcy. That's what he'd wanted so badly for them. A series of moments, actually. Just the day-to-day aspects of love. Renting some movies, having some burgers, a daily kiss in the coffee shop. . .

But that was never Gaia's life. Everything had always been drama. Everything had always been life or death. Everything had always been jam-packed with confusion and doubt and betrayal. That was why Ed had finally given up—because she could never just *be* there with him like that. There was always something else or some*one* else making things a hundred times more complicated.

But if Ed had believed that Gaia was capable of that kind of normal life, if he had believed back then that she was capable of having moments like that perfectly normal kiss with Jake, then he never would have given up on her in the first place.

It was the irony. The stupid, pointless irony. That was what was pissing him off. That was what kept images of Gaia Moore running through his head long after he'd gotten over her.

Kai suddenly plopped down in Ed's lap and wrapped her arms around his neck. "Did you score it?"

"What?" Ed asked absentmindedly.

"My sweet, sweet spare," Kai boasted joyfully. "Did you see it?"

"Oh, yeah. I mean, no. I was just about to—"

"Ed, were you watching me at all?" Kai poked her finger into his head.

"Was I. . . ? Of *course.*" He smiled. "Of course I was watching you."

"Okay, what pins did I hit?"

Oh God, not a test. Come on. "You hit. . . the pins to pick up the spare."

"*Ugggh.*" Kai clenched her fists and shook them with mock frustration. But Ed could tell it wasn't exactly mock frustration.

"What?" Ed laughed, trying desperately to keep things light.

"You're driving me *crazy* today."

"Why?"

Kai looked deeper into Ed's eyes as if to say, *Are you kidding me?*

"What?"

Kai removed her arms from around Ed's neck and crossed them over her chest. The expression on her face was turning `far too serious`. It made Ed nervous. "Ed. . . do you want to talk about our little 'moment' at Starbucks today?"

Ed felt his chest begin to tighten. "What moment?"

Kai blew out a small, uncomfortable sigh. She

turned away from him for a moment and then turned back. "Okay. Let me rephrase. Do you want to talk about Gaia?" Ed was beginning to feel a little sick. "Because sometimes that helps," Kai went on. "Sometimes it helps to get someone out of your system if you just talk a little about—"

"No," Ed interrupted. "What are you *talking* about? Out of my system? Don't be ridiculous. Gaia Moore is so utterly and completely out of my system."

"Well, you just seem so preoccupied with—"

"God, I don't know what you're talking about." He laughed. "Preoccupied? You don't get it. Oh, man, you've got it completely wrong. You want to know why I was just so preoccupied? You want to know why I missed your spare?"

"Why?"

"Because I was feeling jealous."

This didn't make Kai happier. "I know that," she said quietly. "I know you were jealous at Starbucks—"

"*No,* not jealous of *Jake.* Jealous of *them.*" Ed pointed out to the rest of the bowling couples. "I was watching them. They've all been kissing this entire time, and I was jealous. Because that should be *us.* We should be kissing after every strike and every spare and every gutter ball. That's what we should be doing."

The smile suddenly crept back across Kai's face. "Oh," she uttered quietly.

Ed ran his hand up along Kai's cheek and then

75

cradled her chin, pulling her face closer to his until their lips connected. Gently at first, and then firmer and firmer—probing each other's lips with force and with passion.

Now it ought to be crystal clear who Ed was thinking about tonight. He wasn't thinking about Gaia, he was thinking about Kaia.

Kai. He was thinking about *Kai.*

Another
false home—
another room
with
another bed, **home**
for a
short while, **sweet**
until **home**
things
changed
again.

THE TAXICAB WAS FAIRLY NEW. THAT

Headaches and Homelessness

was good, because Gaia felt sick. Nothing too major—just a headache—but she was grateful for the clean vinyl smell and the fresh New York air blowing into the cab. The driver wasn't making things any more pleasant—he was madly speeding up and slowing down—but Gaia could take it.

"How are you feeling?" Jake asked.

Gaia didn't feel like answering. She was tired, and her head hurt. She had her eyes closed, with her head resting on the smooth flaps of the cardboard box in her lap. She said, "Mmm," and hoped he would understand: not great, but fine.

Jake's hand squeezed her shoulder for a second and then pulled away. He understood. She didn't want to talk. He also understood that she'd hurt her arm; Gaia could tell by the gentle way he touched her. She was beginning to like that about Jake: he caught on to things. He didn't make a big deal about it, but he kept his eyes open.

Just a few boxes, Gaia thought. *That's all my life comes down to, really.*

It was true. She had her clothes—really just a

collection of worn-out T-shirts, sweatshirts, and jeans—and what passed for her "toiletries" and a few pairs of shoes, all in a garbage bag on her lap. Jake, next to her, held another, heavier box, with her schoolbooks and a few other things. He had insisted on taking the heavy box, and Gaia hadn't stopped him. He had a point: after that crazy, inexplicable fight she still felt weak. In the cab's trunk were two more boxes. And that was it. That was all it took to relocate Gaia Moore from East Seventy-second Street to her new home.

"Still got that headache?"

"Yeah."

"That was one hell of a fight." Jake was keeping his voice low—but he sounded almost excited. He wanted to talk about that freak show. "How could they *move* like that? The guy who tried to stab me was so *fast*."

He sure was, Gaia thought. *Any faster and you'd be dead.*

"We creamed them, though," Jake went on. "Two against—what was it, *seven*? I mean, I'd give us a pretty high score, given the odds."

"Eight," Gaia said. She wanted him to stop talking, but she couldn't say that. "It was eight. And we barely made it, Jake. What the hell were they on? What was their *deal*?"

"So how would you score us?"

"I *wouldn't*," Gaia said, sitting up straight and looking at him. "I don't keep score. This isn't a *game*." *It's*

79

my life, she thought bitterly. *Assassins and headaches and homelessness and welcome to it.* "You almost got *killed*, Jake. This wasn't some sparring exercise."

"All right." Jake had his hand back on her shoulder. His head was backlit by the streetlights; she could see his chiseled profile as he glanced at her. "All right, sorry."

"I didn't mean to snap at you," Gaia said. "But that freaked me out, Jake. Those kids were so messed up. Did you see their eyes? And the stuff they were yelling about 'God'?"

"That was crazy," Jake said. He was leaning forward, looking at the buildings they were passing. Gaia realized she'd hurt his feelings. He was adrenalized and injured, and he wanted to have a bonding conversation about their side-by-side fighting skills, like they were some kind of dynamic duo. It wasn't his fault. It was all new to him.

And there's fear, she reminded herself. *He got scared. This is how he deals with it—acting like it was a PlayStation game and not a real knife cutting his shirt open.*

She always forgot to take fear into account. She forgot to translate into everyone else's language.

"Jake," Gaia said. She reached out and touched his sleeve. "I'm glad you weren't hurt. I'm glad you were there, fighting with me."

Jake smiled. He seemed embarrassed—and then he

suddenly leaned forward. "Up here, driver," he yelled. "That big brownstone."

They were on Bank Street already, Gaia saw. The taxicab cruised to a stop. She got the door open and climbed out, holding her box of clothes, while Jake paid the driver. She looked over at the brownstone.

It wasn't bad, Gaia thought. She had to admit it; her new home—the Collingwood Residency Hall (a fancy way of saying "boardinghouse," she knew)—looked nice. It was an old-fashioned six-story brownstone with ornate columns, bright windows, and a wide set of stone steps that led up to a dark mahogany front door.

But she didn't want to be here. Another false home—another room with another bed, for a short while, until things changed again. Gaia thought about other high school students, who complained about going home to their parents' houses, about rules they had to follow, about their annoying younger brothers and sisters. All they did was complain.

But it didn't sound so bad. To Gaia, it sounded like a dream come true.

"Come on, Gaia!"

Jake had the boxes from the trunk—he was already bounding up the steps, the boxes stacked up in his arms. Trying to look strong, Gaia thought. Like he wasn't hurt—like he didn't have a gash in his shirt and a big bruise on his bicep and dried blood all over his knuckles from the fight.

81

The doorbell rang loudly, deep in the brownstone. Gaia heard footsteps clattering around and saw shadows moving on the curtains. She could hear voices approaching.

Please don't let this suck, she thought. *Please let this be a halfway decent place.*

The door swung open.

A tall, slender Japanese woman stood in the bright hallway. It was one of the cleanest, neatest spaces Gaia had ever seen. There was a dark hardwood floor and lemon yellow wallpaper. Gaia could hear footsteps pounding on the ceiling above; someone else was home.

The woman wore a beige business suit over a white shirt with a tightly fastened collar. She was smiling ferociously.

"Gaia!" the woman said warmly. She had a very mild accent. "So good to meet you finally. I am Suko—Suko Wattanabe. Please, come in. So many boxes," she added.

"Thanks," Gaia said, forcing herself to smile. "I'm Gaia. This is Jake."

"Hey." Jake's face was blocked by the boxes. He stepped forward.

"No, no," Suko said quickly. She had raised a hand, as if warding off traffic. "I'm sorry; the rule here is that boys are not allowed."

Here we go, Gaia thought. Her heart was sinking. *Here's where it starts sucking. And I'm not even in the front door.*

"He's got to help me with the boxes," Gaia said. "He can come in the front door, can't he?"

Suko smiled, but the smile didn't affect her eyes—they stared back at Gaia, reflecting the orangy streetlights. "I'm sorry; the rule's pretty strict," she said—apologetically, as if it were all out of her hands. "Jason, just put the boxes down; one of the other girls will help."

Jake was putting the boxes down. Suko noticed the slit in his shirt and the dried blood then—she seemed startled. But she recovered fast, turning her smile back to Gaia. She put out her hand, very primly, to shake.

Come on, Gaia, she told herself. *Make this work.*

"Hello, Ms. Wattanabe," Gaia said. "It's nice to meet you."

Suko beamed. "It's a pleasure to make your acquaintance, Gaia. I'm sure your stay with us will be a pleasant one. We'll have plenty of time to—ah!"

Suko turned expectantly. Someone was clumping loudly down the stairs. Gaia and Jake looked over.

A girl descended into view. Gaia saw her shoes first—expensive, gleaming Robert Clergerie shoes. Then she saw a plaid skirt, like a girls' school uniform.

It *was* a girls' school uniform, Gaia realized, although it was artfully disheveled and sloppy. The girl galloping down the stairs was tall and skinny, with long blond hair. She wore a tartan skirt with a pin holding it shut, but the top of the uniform was replaced by an oversized Eminem T-shirt. Gaia saw a small gold stud on the side of her nose.

As she came down into view, the new girl looked over curiously at Gaia and Jake. Mostly at Jake.

"Zan, this is Gaia Moore," Suko said warmly. Her gestures were very formal, and she never seemed to stop smiling. "She'll be joining us."

"Great." Zan looked right at Gaia. Her face suggested that it was anything but. Her gaze went from Gaia's head to her feet and back up. Blatantly sizing her up.

Gaia stared right back.

"Please," Suko said, "would you help Gaia with her boxes?"

Zan took a second. She kept looking at Gaia with the same regal look, like she was Scarlett O'Hara coming down the staircase in a southern mansion for a great ball. Then she turned and smiled tightly at Suko. The smile didn't look very genuine.

"Sure," Zan said.

This is a girl who doesn't like to take orders, Gaia realized. *And I don't think she likes lifting boxes, either.*

But she was obeying.

"I can manage," Gaia said quickly. "It's really no trouble."

Zan took the top box from the floor in front of Jake. She got very close to him to do it. "You notice she didn't introduce you," Zan said. She flipped her hair back from her face as she smiled at him. "So I don't know your name."

84

"Um—" Jake had nothing to say. Suko was watching carefully—she seemed determined that Jake not move a single inch into the building.

"No boys allowed," Zan told Gaia. It was friendly enough, but Gaia suspected that she was making a show for Jake's benefit. "You heard that, right?"

"Yeah."

"Zan, please show Gaia into the front room with the window," Suko said. "Jason, we can manage the boxes."

"I'm Jake," he told her. "Gaia, um—"

"I'm sorry," Gaia told him. Her headache was still there, throbbing dully behind her forehead. She stepped over and kissed him quickly and then hugged him. Zan was carrying one of Gaia's boxes up the stairs.

"I'm sorry, Jake," she repeated. Suddenly she felt very alone and very, very tired. "I'm sorry you can't come in."

"Not your fault," Jake said. He put his hands on her shoulders, looking down at her face, concerned. "You sure you're all right? You want me to buy you a cup of coffee or something?"

"I just want to sleep," Gaia said. She knew what he was really saying. He wanted to talk. But there was no way. She was barely ready for that conversation, even if she'd been wide awake.

"All right," Jake said. "So, take it easy. I'll see you tomorrow."

"Yeah." She squeezed his hand. "Thanks, Jake. Thanks for—"

Fighting next to me? Nearly getting killed? Patiently waiting while I put off our "big conversation"? Carrying my boxes? Obeying the stupid rules of this place? Saving my life? Again? Understanding that I can't talk yet?

"—everything. Thanks for everything."

Jake smiled. "Sure."

Then he nodded at Suko and turned around and walked down the wide stone stairs into the night. Gaia watched his dark silhouette move down Bank Street and out of view.

He'd do anything for me, Gaia realized. *Anything.*

So why can't I talk to him? Why can't I give him what he's asking for?

Gaia didn't know.

"Well!" Suko was swinging the wide mahogany door shut. She seemed visibly relieved now that the threat of a male intruder had passed. "I'm sure you want to settle in, Gaia. Zan will help you. Dinner is at seven sharp," she added. Suko turned the door's locks, and the harsh sound echoed through the gleaming room.

"Thanks," Gaia said.

She felt like crying suddenly. She had no idea why—it came out of nowhere. Gaia squinted for a moment and concentrated and it passed, and she felt fine again. An old habit. But she was trying to force things to be *right,* to be bearable. . . and it wasn't working.

Come on, Gaia, she told herself. *Time to be new Gaia. There's nothing wrong with this place. There's nothing wrong with Jake. There's no reason to be angry.* She turned and followed Zan up the stairs.

A Bare, Clean Mattress

"HERE YOU GO," ZAN SAID. "HOME sweet home and all that."

Gaia looked through the door. She could see a very small bedroom. It was so narrow that the bed took up nearly the entire room. Gaia could tell, looking at the walls, that it had once been part of a much larger room—it had been partitioned off. There was a tiny wooden desk with a bright shaded lamp, and, at the other end of the narrow bed, a big window showing nothing but black night.

There were no posters. There were no pictures or any decoration at all. The bed was unmade—a bare, clean mattress with sheets and blankets piled at one end. The floor was gleaming bare floorboards. A streetlight outside shone yellow on the bare ceiling.

"Great," Gaia said. She tried not to project any sarcasm, but it didn't work. "Thank you, Zan."

"No worries." Zan was putting down the box she'd carried upstairs. She grunted with the effort. "What the hell is in here—rocks?"

"Some books."

"Anyway, that's me." Zan was pointing at the next doorway. "If you need anything."

Gaia caught a glimpse of another, larger bedroom. The streetlight shone in the window, illuminating a Massive Attack poster. "Okay."

Zan followed Gaia into her tiny bedroom. Gaia went over to the window, peering out into the darkness. She could see the bright streetlamp and the shadows of the trees on the street. "So was that your boyfriend downstairs?" Zan asked. "He's a little bit cute."

"He's—" Zan had asked a very good question, Gaia realized. What *was* Jake, anyway? "He's my friend. I'm not sure."

"Uh-huh."

"Too bad he couldn't come in."

Zan frowned, squinting. "There are ways."

Gaia sat down on the bed. It was very firm. She could hear the springs creaking.

"So, you like to party?" Zan asked.

"Um—sometimes, I guess." It was a lame answer, but Gaia had no idea what to say. There was just no way to explain her life to this girl. And what Gaia really wanted to do was *sleep*—at least at that moment. Her headache was just beginning to fade.

Looking at Zan, Gaia realized she'd given the wrong answer. Zan was already bored with her.

"If Suko tells you to do something, just do it," Zan said.

"So you can't break any of her rules?"

Zan smirked. "Like I said, there are ways," she said.

Then she left the room, and Gaia started unpacking.

Claustrophobic

"TONIGHT WE ARE HAVING TERIYAKI," Suko said. "I have made it for this special occasion—a new guest has joined our little family."

This isn't my family, Gaia thought. *That's not what the word means.*

The dining room was big and bright, lit by soft white lamps behind Japanese screens against the walls. The floor was covered by a straw-colored mat.

Gaia moved toward her chair, and then they all sat down. The big oak table was surrounded by empty chairs. There was nobody there but Suko and Zan and another girl at the other end of the table. She wore thick glasses and a pink shirt. Nobody had introduced her.

The whole scene was strange—and, Gaia thought glumly, she had to get used to it, because as long as her father was away, this was home. There was nothing to be gained by getting these people angry with her. She had to make it work. It was just a boardinghouse, after all—it wasn't like anyone was torturing her. They were serving her dinner, weren't they? The smells from the kitchen weren't half bad.

"Thanks," Gaia said.

Suko somehow managed to frown at her while still smiling. Gaia didn't know very many people who could do that.

Zan laughed.

Gaia looked over at her, startled. The laugh had been very loud. Zan seemed beside herself—she was covering her mouth, trying not to laugh more.

What's so funny? Gaia wondered.

The white kitchen door opened. An elderly Japanese man came in, wearing a blue apron with Japanese writing on it and holding a tray of covered platters. When he saw Gaia, he smiled, nodding slightly. Gaia nodded back.

"Gaia, here at Collingwood we have many activities for our guests," Suko was saying. "I personally give lectures on the martial arts, if you are interested. I am a black belt, trained by. . . Well, you know."

Suko seemed reluctant to mention the Agency, as if

she didn't want to break the illusion that this was just another girls' boardinghouse. As she spoke, the old man was carefully laying out the platters and taking the covers off. "When he is not cooking, Philip also gives talks about the history of the romantic period in literature. Zan, please."

"Sorry," Zan said. She had still been laughing; her face was red.

Gaia smiled politely.

"I'm sorry, too," Zan went on. "Gaia and me—we're both sorry."

There was something strange about Zan—about the way she was acting. Something strange about the way her face looked. Gaia couldn't put her finger on what it was, but it was quite different from the way she'd been upstairs.

"Are there other girls living here?" Gaia asked Suko.

Suko nodded enthusiastically. "Zan you have met. Her father also is busy, working for the federal government, as your father is. Alexa, at the end of the table, is the daughter of a—"

"Shooting people," Zan said loudly. "Dad's in the Middle East, shooting people in secret. That's his gig. That's—"

"Zan!" Suko was sitting bolt upright, glaring at Zan. "Please!"

"Why he can't be home for Christmas or Thanksgiving or my birthday. What?"

91

The doorbell rang. Gaia recognized the sound from earlier, when Jake had rung it. It was a loud electric buzzer.

"You're being impolite," Suko told her. The clanking of silverware went on as Philip continued to move around the table, serving each of them. "We've discussed this. Alexa, would you get the door, please? And explain that we're eating."

"May I be excused?" Zan said.

She's high, Gaia realized suddenly. *She's high on something.*

Now that Gaia had figured it out, she was sure that was what was making Zan's pretty face look so strange. Her pupils were expanded, like black basketballs. Her face was flushed. Her movements were exaggerated.

Alexa, the quiet girl in the pink shirt, had stood up; she was folding her napkin, heading out of the room to answer the door.

"No, Zan—you must eat with us. There aren't special rules for you," Suko said patiently. "Gaia, I'll explain the rules to you in detail later. There's a curfew each night that you have to obey—that's one thing. We like to have everyone accounted for by 10 P.M. on weeknights, 11 P.M. on weekends."

"But—" Gaia was beginning to feel physically claustrophobic, like she was locked in a closet. Philip had ambled around the table and was doling out fragrant beef teriyaki for her. "I'm sorry, but I can't understand why—"

"*See* her! I need to see Gaia Moore right now!"

The loud male voice came from the front door. Now they all could hear it.

And Gaia realized that she recognized the voice. She knew it very well.

The bright light shone on Oliver's face, and for a moment Gaia was shocked **hidden in shadow** at how much he looked like Loki.

OLIVER COULDN'T MAKE HEADS OR

Family Emergency

tails of it. He was convinced that those men had no more been CIA than they were space aliens. But they'd wanted to know about the serum—and they'd wanted to know about Gaia. And that meant they'd be looking for her and trying to ask her the same questions they'd asked him.

Gaia was tough—Oliver knew that better than almost anyone on earth. But she could be caught unawares. She could be surprised. She could be *fooled*—that was the approach that had worked best for him when he'd been Loki. It was easier to fool a young girl than it was a mature adult. Play to her emotions, threaten her loved ones. . . it was simple. And she could be overcome by force if you had enough men willing to endure broken bones. She wasn't invincible.

But you couldn't scare her.

Which was too bad, Oliver thought. Sometimes it was *good* to be scared. It gave you a sense of what was dangerous and what to avoid. And it kept you from doing anything stupid, like trying to fight a huge organization single-handed. A girl born without the fear gene was still vulnerable—even more so.

"I'm sorry, sir," the girl in the pink shirt was saying.

The streetlight reflected on her thick glasses. "I can't let you until the governess—"

"I'm her *uncle*," Oliver snapped. "Her father is out of town on business—that's why she's here. I need to speak to her. It's—it's a family emergency."

"Sir—"

"I need to *see* her!" Oliver hadn't meant to raise his voice, but he was losing his patience. "I need to see Gaia Moore right now! Damn it, it's *important*!"

"Oliver."

He stopped talking and stared past the girl in the pink shirt. He knew that voice very well.

It was Gaia. She was standing in the vestibule next to a wide white staircase. A Japanese woman in a business suit stood behind her, and—in a doorway, back in the distance—Oliver could just see another blond girl, leaning into the vestibule, staring at him in frank curiosity.

"Oliver, what's going on?"

She wasn't hurt. Oliver was so relieved, he nearly sank to the ground.

"Gaia," Oliver said, stepping past the girl into the building. "Gaia, I'm so sorry to bother you here, but there's been a—"

"Stop, please," the Japanese woman said. She had held up her hand like a crossing guard. "Sir, no guests are allowed without authorization—and certainly no male guests."

"I'm her uncle," Oliver said doggedly. "I have to speak with my niece *now*."

"Can't you just give us a moment?" Gaia asked the woman. "Please, Suko."

"The rules are—"

As Oliver watched, Gaia leaned to whisper in the Japanese woman's ear. Oliver strained to hear, but he couldn't. The Japanese woman listened, looking avidly at Oliver. And she started to nod.

"SUKO, COULD YOU PLEASE ALLOW

Safe

an exception to the rule?" Gaia whispered. "He's my uncle, and he wouldn't be here if it wasn't important. It's my first night here. Please?"

Gaia didn't feel comfortable pleading. But she really wanted to hear what Oliver had to say. It was so strange—his showing up out of the blue and insisting on talking—that she was determined to listen to him. Sometimes begging was the only option.

Suko nodded slowly, staring at Oliver. It seemed to be working.

"Just let me talk to him for a couple of minutes," Gaia went on. She was sure Oliver couldn't hear her— he was too far away. "Then I'll get rid of him—I'll talk him into leaving."

97

"All right," Suko said dubiously. She nodded at Oliver, smiling. "Gaia will step outside and speak with you on the front steps. But just for a few minutes."

"Hey, no fair," Zan pointed out sullenly from behind them.

"Thanks, Suko."

"Yes—thank you," Oliver said gratefully.

Gaia stepped out onto the boardinghouse's front landing. The night air was cool. She pulled Collingwood's thick door shut behind her. Now they were standing in darkness. Oliver's face was hidden in shadow; she saw just a halo of orange streetlamp light shining around his head.

"Oliver, what's—"

"Thank God you're safe," Oliver said. "Tom never told me where he was sending you. I've spent the entire day just trying to track you down." He reached out as if to hug her, but he seemed embarrassed. He took her hand, squeezing it awkwardly before letting it go.

"What do you mean, 'safe'? What happened?"

"I was writing you a letter," Oliver began, and then started over. "Two men. Two men came to my house this morning, claiming to be CIA agents. They tried to interrogate me."

Gaia was confused. "Didn't the CIA already debrief you about—?"

"*Yes*," Oliver said sharply. He had seized her arm. "But this was different. That's my point, Gaia. They

98

weren't real CIA. They *couldn't* have been. They were giving me an act, but I saw right through it."

"Oliver, are you sure they weren't CIA?" Gaia asked carefully. "I mean, they could have had some follow-up questions."

"Of *course* I'm sure," Oliver said harshly. "Do you think I'm a fool? They wanted to know about you, about the awful things I'd done to you in the past. They wanted lab records and doctors' logs. They wanted to know about that serum. You remember the serum?"

Gaia remembered. Looking up at the dark shadow of Oliver's face, looming over her, she remembered vividly. She remembered the straps that had held her down, and she remembered this man—her uncle— carefully, brilliantly lying to her.

But that was all in the past.

"These two cut-rate gunmen came to my house with an absurd story and tried to get me to talk about you, Gaia. I refused, but they wouldn't listen, and I had to attack them before they would leave."

"You *attacked* them?" Gaia's heart was sinking. "Oliver, that's exactly the kind of thing that can get you in trouble with the Agency. You're supposed to be on your best behavior. Don't you understand that they're watching you like hawks?"

Behind Gaia the front door was creaking open. The bright light shone on Oliver's face, and for a moment Gaia was shocked at how much he looked like Loki. It was a baleful stare of frustration that she remembered well.

Suko was standing there, smiling. "Excuse me," she said. "But it is time now for Gaia to return inside."

"Gaia," Oliver said—and now he looked like a tired, confused man and not like a criminal mastermind at all—"I know they're watching me. I know I have to be on my best behavior. But I'm no fool. And I think you're in trouble again. Big trouble. We all are."

Please, Gaia thought weakly. *Please don't do this. Please don't pull me back into that world, Oliver. Into that life.*

"Gaia, please come in now," Suko whispered behind her.

It was time to go back into the boardinghouse.

And the thing was, it suddenly didn't seem so bad. Even with the druggie prep-school girl and the curfews, it wasn't so bad at all. She just had to get used to it.

"I think you should come with me tonight. I can protect you better than this—" He gestured at the building behind them.

"No." Gaia didn't even have to think about it. There wasn't the slightest chance she would do that. "I'm sorry, Oliver. But I can't. I'm trying to get *away* from all that, don't you understand? After the Yuri thing I'm even more determined than ever to get

100

away from all of it—to start living a normal life."

"We all want that," Oliver said. "It's a nice fairy tale, but it's impossible. Come with me, Gaia," he repeated. He was openly pleading now. "Please."

I have a choice. It was amazing how clear her head was suddenly.

"No," Gaia said. "I'm sorry, Oliver, but I can't. I have to stay here."

"They weren't real CIA," Oliver insisted. "Gaia, you've got to believe me."

Behind Gaia, Suko was waiting. She seemed to recoil from Oliver's harsh tone.

"I'll be safe here," Gaia promised. "Don't worry, Oliver. The Agency set this place up. It's a safe house. Suko's a black belt."

"That is true," Suko said primly.

"Please go, Oliver," Gaia said gently. She reached up to touch his arm. "I'm really grateful for your concern. But it's. . . it's curfew. Right, Suko?"

Oliver looked down at her, and his expression was difficult to read. A blending of scorn and concern and love. And regret.

Then he turned away into the night. Gaia watched `his stooped, beaten figure` walking away. And then, with Suko smiling at her, she turned and went inside.

She didn't even scan the street to see if anyone was watching—she was sure that she was safe.

NIGHT HAD FALLEN.

Heather knew because the speaking clock in the lounge told her what time it was. She had no other way to tell.

A Cold Voice

For Heather Gannis, it was always pretty much night. The darkness was endless. For ages—for days, weeks, months—Heather had been completely blind, and a clock with a mechanical voice told her whether it was night or day.

So the darkness couldn't really increase her fear. But this night she was already so frightened that it didn't matter.

She didn't even want to think about the day she'd just had. She remembered it all—the voices, the questions, the fear. . . . She was so scared, she was still shivering, even though the room was warm. She couldn't help it.

The visitors had come early that afternoon. Right after lunch, in fact. Heather had taken her tray up to the counter—they all knew how to do that at the school without running into each other—and had navigated back to her room, following the edges of the walls as she always did.

And someone had been there.

It was obvious from the way the air felt. Heather came through her doorway, all ready to fall onto her bed and take a catnap, and she realized she wasn't alone.

"Hello?" Heather called out. "Hello?"

"Heather," Mrs. Delgado said, "don't worry. Everything's fine."

Mrs. Delgado was the superintendent of the school. Immediately Heather was nervous. What was the superintendent doing in her room? Furthermore, why was she insisting that everything was fine? People only said stuff like that when it wasn't true.

And, Heather realized, there were other people in the room. And a smell of aftershave or cologne that she didn't recognize. After all the months of blindness, Heather didn't make mistakes about things like that. She *knew* there were strangers in the room.

"Heather, these men need to talk to you," Mrs. Delgado went on. "I have no idea what it's about, but it would be a good idea to just answer their questions as best you can."

Mrs. Delgado sounded scared. Heather was sure of it. Being blind gave you a built-in lie detector. And an emotion detector, too. And Delgado was terrified—there was no question about it.

"You can leave now," a male voice said.

It was a cold voice, and Heather didn't recognize it. She felt the air move as Mrs. Delgado got up; she heard footsteps on floorboards and carpet as the superintendent hurried past Heather, squeezing her shoulder reassuringly and then moving toward the door and pulling it shut.

Click. That was the door latch. Heather was alone, with the strangers.

"Hello?" she said again. "Who's there?"

"Heather," the strange male voice said again, "My name is James Rowan. The other person you're hearing is Peter Morrow."

"Okay," Heather said dubiously.

"You're a very pretty young lady," Rowan said. It sounded strange to Heather. Because she never thought about how people looked anymore. It was utterly irrelevant.

"Why don't you have a seat," the other man said. "We just have a few questions and we'll be out of your hair."

"Who are you?" Heather said. Her heart was beating so fast, she could hear it clicking in her ears. She was absolutely terrified, she realized.

"You don't need to worry about that," Rowan said. He was closer to the window, and the breeze was blowing his cologne across Heather's face. Old Spice, she realized. Who the hell wore Old Spice, anyway? "You might say we're investigators."

"You mean police?" Heather remembered how frightened Mrs. Delgado had sounded and realized that these men must have shown her a badge of some kind. Or a gun.

"Don't be afraid," Morrow said. It was like he'd read her mind. "We're not cops. We're employees of a government agency. We're really just bureaucrats. We're certainly not dangerous."

He's lying, Heather realized. *They're dangerous as hell.*

"We'd like to talk to you about your affliction. Your blindness," Rowan explained needlessly.

"I know what 'affliction' means."

"Now, there's no need to be difficult," Morrow said. Heather could tell from his voice that he was smiling. "Are you going to have an attitude? It will just make this take longer and be more unpleasant for you."

"N-No."

"You were made blind by an injected drug?" Rowan asked.

What? Heather was confused. *Why are they asking about that? How do they even know about that?*

"I don't really know what it was," Heather said truthfully. "I'd rather not talk about it."

"Did you go blind all at once, or did it happen in stages?"

"It was the last stage," Heather said.

"Was the first stage fearlessness?" Rowan asked. He seemed particularly eager to hear her answer. "Were you fearless? No fear at all?"

"Yes."

Heather remembered it vividly. That strange, exhilarating sensation—that unreal, dreamlike disconnection of having no fear. And then later. . . the burning pain, the fever. . . the fear of not understanding.

And then blackness.

"Heather," Morrow went on, "did you undergo any kind of examination or blood test during that first stage?"

"No."

"You answered awfully quickly," Rowan said. "It's been a long time since the events we're discussing. Are you *sure*? Absolutely *sure* there was no blood test? Even by a paramedic or an emergency-room nurse?"

"Nothing like that," Heather insisted. "It just happened so *quickly*. There was no time for that."

Rowan sighed in frustration. Heather heard it clearly.

"And Gaia Moore?" Morrow asked suddenly. "Did she receive the same injection?"

"I don't understand," Heather said. She heard the fear in her voice and tried to suppress it. "You *caught* him, didn't you? The man who did this to me? Oliver Moore? You caught him. Why don't you ask *him* all these questions?"

"Because we're asking you," Morrow said.

"Answer the question, Heather," Rowan went on. "And you'd better be sure you're answering truthfully."

Heather was so frightened that she could barely speak. But at the same time, she was irritated. She'd been following the conversation very closely. It was amazing how well you could pay attention to things when you weren't distracted by appearances, facial expressions, colors.

And these men weren't being truthful. Heather had no idea what the lie was, but there was a lie in there somehow. Their voices gave it away.

"I don't know," Heather insisted. "I don't know what they did to her. He'd been making her life hell for months."

Rowan was standing up. The sound filled Heather with relief. *The interview is over,* she thought. *Thank God—they're leaving.*

But she was wrong.

Rowan came right over to stand in front of her. The smell of Old Spice was overpowering. Heather could hear him breathing.

And then she felt the man's hand on her shoulder.

"Please stop," Heather whispered. "Please leave me alone."

"We'll go," Rowan said, "if you swear to us that you've told us the truth. And that there's *nothing* you've left out. About the injection, Ms. Moore, any of it."

"I swear," Heather whispered. She was crying—she couldn't help it. "I swear. Please leave me alone. Please."

"One more thing," Rowan said. He pushed his hand downward on her shoulder. "Don't tell *anybody* about us. That superintendent, your teachers, anyone. If you do, we'll find out. And we'll come back. Do you understand?"

"Yes."

"Good girl."

And then suddenly they were gone. She felt the hand lift from her shoulder. Then she heard the door opening and closing and the footsteps, and she was alone in her room with the cloying smell of Old Spice lingering in the air.

And now, three hours later, Heather sat in the lounge, trembling. She hadn't said a word to anyone. She'd taken a shower, and put on clean pajamas, and eaten dinner, and now she was sitting quietly in the lounge.

I've got to tell someone, Heather thought.

`It was exactly what they had told her not to do.`

But she had to. She had to at least ask someone for advice. Maybe not help, but advice. It wasn't like they were going to spy on her. And she had to figure out what to do next.

Not somebody at the school. That was a bad idea. She needed to talk to someone she really knew— someone she could trust.

And more importantly, she had to warn Gaia.

I've got to tell someone. I've got to ask someone what to do. But who?

And suddenly Heather made up her mind. She knew exactly who to call.

FIELD REPORT: INTERVIEW WITH SUBJECT A-3-B

Rowan, J., and Morrow, P., reporting

Interview was conducted at 6:20 P.M. EST. The subject, Heather Gannis (see attached file 31), appeared to be cooperating and answering questions truthfully. The subject's blindness called for innovative interrogation/intimidation techniques.

As with Oliver Moore (see Field Report A-2-A), the interview proved somewhat inconclusive. However, certain clear conclusions may be drawn. The test subject appeared to have a detailed memory of the events in question regarding BLUEBELL, our code name for the genetic serum administered in the sequence of events under scrutiny.

The lack of alkaloid agents has been tentatively confirmed, as has the absence of sensory side effects concurrent with injection.

School Superintendent Marisa Delgado was easily persuaded to hand over all of Heather Gannis's medical records, which revealed the drug's effects quite clearly. The blindness is a side effect of the antigen-reagent properties of the serum. No further information may be garnered from Heather Gannis.

The investigation must proceed to its main subject, who, it has been revealed, is in the process of being contacted. Rowan and Morrow shall proceed as ordered; a subsequent field report will be submitted thereafter through the usual channels.

END

Old Gaia
would have
checked out
this scene
and
turned
right
back around
in a
heartbeat.

the
beautiful
people

"JAKE! JAKE!"

Like Bullets

It was a girl's voice calling out to him, but Jake couldn't see her face in the crowd. He saw Gaia first as he stepped out of the school lobby. She saw him, too, and smiled—but she wasn't the one calling to him. It was the girl next to her—the girl in the long white leather coat. She called his name again, waving. Jake finally realized that it was that girl he'd seen on his way out of Starbucks. Liz.

The last buzzer was still echoing through the lobby behind Jake. School was over, and now he was surrounded by a stream of dozens of students with book bags, yelling back and forth to each other and hollering on their cell phones as they flooded out of the school building.

"Jake!" Liz yelled again. Her flawless white teeth gleamed as she smiled at him. The afternoon sunlight lit up the gold strands of her hair.

Jake moved through the flood of kids and made his way over to Gaia and Liz. He gave Gaia a kiss and tipped his chin at Liz.

"Are you coming to my party?" Liz asked immediately.

"Party?" Jake asked. "What party? When is it?"

"It's right now." Liz grinned.

"Liz and Chris booked a suite over at the Mercer Hotel," Gaia explained.

Jake knew where that was—a fancy building a few blocks west—but he'd never been inside the place.

"I think they pretty much invited. . . everybody," Gaia went on. "How many, Liz?"

Gaia sounded like she was trying to seem disinterested. But Jake knew better. It was obvious—Gaia was intrigued despite herself. He had to hand it to Gaia's friend Liz. She just made it look so easy. She was one of those people who you just liked in a matter of seconds, and you instantly stopped caring about the fact that her wristwatch cost more than most cars.

"Dozens," Liz said, shrugging. "Okay, yes, everyone," she admitted sheepishly. "It's already started—Chris is over there now. I stayed behind to gather the stragglers. Like *you* Jake."

Liz poked Jake in the chest as she said his name. It was completely innocent and friendly, and he didn't mind at all.

Neither did Gaia. It was obvious, looking at her. Gaia seemed to trust Liz completely after only a day. Which made Jake even more impressed with the immaculately dressed newcomer. If she could win Gaia over that fast, then Liz had to be "good people." Gaia didn't waste her time with people she didn't like. It was one of the things Jake liked about her.

"Ready to go, Jake?" Gaia asked.

"Sure," Jake said honestly. "A party at three in the afternoon: Why not? Let's go."

112

"Come on, you two," Liz said impatiently. She grabbed the couple's hands and pulled them forcibly down the street away from the school. "Let's get over there. I just have to buy some beer on the way."

It was a quarter to four when the three of them got to the Mercer Hotel. The tall, graceful building loomed over them, shining in the afternoon sun.

Jake had to admit that the hotel idea was brilliant. He would never have mustered the audacity to try that kind of thing himself. He didn't have the money, either. He wasn't familiar with the Mercer Hotel, but one look at the brass signs and the row of car service limousines lined up in front told him that the place wasn't cheap.

Liz and Jake were both carrying bags from the Korean deli around the corner. Each bag had two six-packs of Stella Artois beer—Liz had insisted on the best the deli had, even if it was something like four dollars a bottle. Jake had tried to pay, but Liz was much quicker, slapping down a fifty-dollar bill before he'd even gotten his hand near his wallet.

"I'm not drinking," Jake told Gaia as they moved through the hotel's revolving doors. The lobby was big and dark and air-conditioned. "I've got a sparring session at the gym in about an hour."

"Okay," Gaia said.

"Just so you know," Jake went on. Liz was leading them toward the banks of elevators; they had to sprint to keep up. "In case you wanted to get me drunk and take advantage of me."

"I stand warned," Gaia replied, cracking a slight smile.

"Come on, lovebirds," Liz called out over her shoulder, as her perfectly manicured index finger stabbed at the elevator button. "I do believe it's party time."

COMING THROUGH THE DOOR INTO The Princely Aura

the hotel suite, Gaia could tell the party was already going full blast. She could hear techno and hip-hop music coming from different directions and an endless cacophony of loud voices. The crowd was right in front of them, packed into the suite's living room, with kids filling the couches and chairs, and opened cans of beer littering the glass coffee table, where a half-circle of kids were loudly playing quarters. Gaia could see doors into other rooms, with more kids moving through them. The suite was huge.

Old Gaia would have checked out this scene and turned right back around in a heartbeat. But this was new Gaia. And so she took a deep breath and tried to immerse herself in the crowd.

But the first face she saw was not making this new commitment to social behavior any easier.

Tannie Deegan. Of course.

"You're *totally* right!" Tannie was squealing. "Oh my God, Chris. You're, like, totally *exactly* right. . . ."

Gaia turned to Liz. "You invited the Friends of Heather?"

"Friends of. . ." Liz squinted in confusion. "Who's Heather?"

"Those girls," Gaia explained. Liz was leading them toward the bedroom, where, sure enough, Gaia could hear the squeals of more FOHs. "From Starbucks yesterday? The vultures."

"Oh God, you're right. It's *them*." Liz looked pained. "I guess Chris must have."

Jake led them through the big white door into the suite's master bedroom. It was a big, bright room with a gigantic king-size bed. A smaller crowd had gathered in the room. A boom box was playing slightly mellower music. A bar to one side held a big bottle of vodka and some mixers and an ice bucket. The air-conditioning was blasting; the room was nice and cool. Out the huge picture window Gaia could see the bright sky and the tops of the buildings near the hotel and, if she craned her neck, a little bit of the river between the buildings in the distance.

Chris Rodke was, without question, the room's center of attention. Gaia recognized him immediately—

the princely aura from the previous day was intact. He was reclining on the wide bed with his shoes off, leaning comfortably on the headboard with a tall glass in one hand. The lamplight shone from his golden yellow hair. Gaia could see the wet frost beading the sides of his glass and the lime and ice. *He's drinking vodka with soda,* Gaia realized. She wasn't sure she'd ever seen anyone under thirty have a vodka and soda.

"That's so *funny,*" Megan gasped. "That's just so funny."

Megan, Tina, and Laura were perched on the soft carpet near Chris. They all had drinks. All of them were laughing as if Chris had made the single most humorous remark in the entire history of human civilization. Gaia thought that Megan was going to pass out, she was laughing so hard.

"Elizabeth Rodke!" Chris yelled out. "'Bout time you made it." When he saw Gaia, he threw his arms around her, then gave her an air kiss on each cheek. "Ga-yah bay-bee," he sang, elongating each syllable.

"Hi, Gaia!" Megan said, far too brightly. "I'm so glad you're here!"

"Right on," Laura squealed.

Gaia blinked two long blinks. *So. . . the attitudes are reversible, just like the Burberry raincoats.*

"Gaia, how the hell are ya?" Chris asked.

"I have no idea," Gaia replied. Too honest, perhaps. She was still working on this stuff. But somehow she'd made Chris smile.

"Oh, Christ, neither do I." Chris laughed. He turned to his sister. "This one's a keeper."

Gaia suddenly realized that the FOHs were watching her like hawks.

"Gaia, come sit with us," Megan suddenly suggested as she tapped a spot on the carpet next to her. Gaia didn't even respond. She could only muster a raised eyebrow of confusion.

"Here," Jake said quietly. He was up close to her, handing over a glass of ice water he'd brought from the bar. He'd gotten himself one, too. "You want to sit down?"

"Sure," she said, moving as far as possible from the disturbing smiles of the FOHs.

"Liz, let's do this every day!" Chris called out. "New party, new hotel." He was finishing his drink—the ice clattered loudly in his glass.

"Oh, *great* idea," Tina squeaked. "Yeah!"

Gaia sat down in an expensive-looking leather chair halfway across the room. Jake dropped onto the carpet beside her.

"So, you live on Fifth?" Megan asked, staring up worshipfully at the Rodkes. She was pivoting on the floor, looking back and forth between the two of them. It must have been hard to decide which one's ass to kiss first. "Do you love it?"

Liz made a face, nodding while she cracked open a beer and sat down. "It's cool. I mean, it's fine. We just

117

got there. Dad's like that—suddenly it's, 'New York, *right now*,' and we have to jump. But the place is nice."

"Right on," Laura said. That seemed to be the sum total of her vocabulary for the day.

Jake slouched on the floor, leaning his head against Gaia's next to her knee.

"*I* love the house," Chris said. "I think it's got great potential."

"Do you have a balcony?" Megan asked. "Overlooking the park?"

"We do," Chris replied.

"Huh. Your place sounds really nice," Megan said. It was fairly obvious that she was fishing for an invite.

"I'm still unpacking boxes," Liz said. It was the perfect answer: a polite refusal to invite anyone anywhere.

Jake pivoted his head, looking up at Gaia. "How are you?" he asked. His hair brushed her knee, making her feel a mild tingle. He was quiet enough that the others didn't seem to hear.

"Fine." Gaia smiled at him. "I'm fine."

He sat up and turned to face her, moving closer.

"I mean. . . do you feel like finishing that conversation?"

Here we go, Gaia thought. She could feel her calm, peaceful mood immediately start to drift away. *He still wants to talk.* After last night's fiasco, she was feeling that much less inclined to have that talk just yet. Last night's sadomasochistic freak show had been the perfect reminder of just exactly why they *shouldn't* have that talk.

118

"There are so many people here," Gaia said. She tried not to sound too evasive, like she was looking for an excuse not to talk to him. The fact that it was true didn't help.

"Big deal," Jake said easily. He was gulping his ice water. "Nobody's listening. We can have a private conversation in the corner and all they'll do is point and giggle."

"True enough," Gaia said. She had a sinking feeling because she couldn't think of a way out this time. Not without actually admitting that she didn't want to talk.

Why not? Let's do it. Let's see what happens when we talk. Let's see if I ruin everything.

Gaia realized she was holding her breath. "Okay," she said, exhaling loudly. "Okay. Let's have that conversation. You're right; this is a perfect time."

"Gaia! Jake!" Chris called out. "Join the party!"

"I've got to work out," Jake said apologetically. "I can't have any—"

"Don't drink, *talk*," Chris went on grandly. "We're new kids; we need to make friends. Gaia, where do you live? Who are you?"

She hated being put on the spot. But something about Chris's way made it a little easier. "I don't really know that, either," she replied honestly. "I'm kind of in transition."

"Who isn't?" Chris joked. "From what to what?"

"Oh," Gaia uttered, thinking it through. "I don't know. . . old to new?"

"*Perfect.*" Chris laughed. "Old to new. Well, here's to the new you, Gaia Moore." He raised his glass. "Not that you need to change anything."

"Yeah, well. . . no one ever really changes, right?"

"Oh, *wrong*," Chris bellowed excitedly. He suddenly shot up off the bed as his eyes widened.

"Oh, *no*, Gaia," Liz moaned. "You've just hit on one of my brother's favorite topics. Please, Chris, no speech. Control yourself."

"Liz, come on," Chris snorted. "They don't even know me yet. They haven't heard some of my best stuff."

Liz turned to Gaia. "Oh God, Gaia, I warned you about my family and speeches. Don't say I never warned you."

"Stop it," Chris complained. "It's not a big deal. Your friend Gaia just happened to say that no one ever changes, and I just wanted to let her know that she was dead wrong, that's all." Chris turned to Gaia like they were sharing a secret. "You're dead wrong."

This Gaia certainly wanted to hear. "Wrong how?"

"No—" Liz giggled, pouncing on her brother to get a hand over his overly verbose mouth.

Chris pushed his sister away in the exact same manner that he probably had since toddlerhood. "Well, as long as you *asked*," he bellowed triumphantly, "I say we're not stuck with anything. Not anything. Not character traits, not physical traits, nothing. I say that we are in complete control. If 'Right On' Laura over here wanted blue eyes, then she could go get color contacts. If Megan were depressed, she'd take Prozac or some other drug. It's all in our hands now. It's all just chemistry."

"Stop, stop," Liz moaned painfully. "Don't you all see where he's going to go with this? Two more seconds and he's going to fall right smack down on his favorite topic: the highly controversial gay gene."

"There's *no such thing*," Chris insisted, pointing at Liz. "No such thing at all. That's a myth. The human chromosome has no gene for gayness."

"*Okay*," Liz moaned again. "I'm not arguing."

"And even if there *was*," Chris went on, "I *still* wouldn't believe in it. I'm gay because I'm gay. It's who I *am*—it's *my choice*. It's the twenty-first century; my genes aren't in charge: I am."

Gaia didn't realize that she was staring at Chris until Jake knocked his hand against her thigh, trying to get her attention. She nodded impatiently at him and turned back to Chris. What he was saying was absolutely fascinating.

My genes aren't in charge: I am.

But Gaia knew that wasn't true. If her life had one unalterable fact, it was this: her genes were in charge of everything. They defined every aspect of her miserable life. What Chris was saying was nonsense.

121

"Chris, how can *you* be in charge?" Gaia argued. "Your genes make you who you are. I took biology; I know how it works."

"How it *usually* works," Chris corrected politely. "The more we learn about heredity, the more in charge we are. Look, you should talk to my dad. He really understands this stuff. The incredible stuff they're doing in some of those labs—it would blow you away."

"I thought your dad made toothpaste," Gaia said.

Chris's eyes widened. "Are you kidding? That's the boring part. They make *everything*. Toothpaste, med supplies, high-end drugs, research—billions of dollars in research. Are you interested in genetics?"

"Well—yeah."

That was one way of putting it. Gaia's entire life had been determined by her own unique genetic code. The funny thing was, Gaia had never really tried to understand it from a scientific standpoint. It had always seemed over her head. But maybe it wasn't.

"Gaia," Jake said, standing up, "I'm leaving."

Gaia looked up at Jake. And suddenly realized she'd been completely ignoring him. Right at the moment that she'd agreed to have the "big conversation." Suddenly she felt awful. Selfish and evasive and awful.

"Jake, I'm so sorry," she said quickly, standing up and taking his hands. "I'm a jerk—I keep stopping you from—"

"Shhh! Relax. It's not you," Jake said smoothly. "It's just that it's getting late. I've got to get to the gym for my sparring session. And I need time to warm up."

"Oh." Gaia looked at Jake's eyes to double-check. "So you're not mad?"

"Mad? No! Of course not. We can talk some other time."

But there was something strange in those eyes— something she'd never seen before.

He's lying, she thought suddenly. *He's lying—he's angry with me. He says he's not, but he is.*

"Are you sure you have to go?" she asked. "You sure you're not mad?"

"Yeah." Jake smiled and lifted his book bag. "Yeah, everything's cool. But I've got to take off."

And then Jake turned around and walked out of the room, his book bag slung from his shoulder. He didn't look back.

That was bad, Gaia thought. *That was really bad. I should go after him—talk to him. So what if they think we're having a fight? So what? I have to fix this.*

She started moving toward the hotel bedroom door. She was about to call out after Jake.

"Hey, Gaia," Chris said, lunging up off the bed. "Why don't you come have dinner?"

"What?"

Gaia turned around and looked at Chris. The FOHs were lined up along the carpet, enviously listening.

They probably would do anything to be invited to the Rodkes' Fifth Avenue apartment.

"Come to dinner," Chris repeated. "Liz was probably going to invite you anyway, right, Liz?"

"You read my mind," Liz said. She smiled at Gaia warmly. "Do come, Gaia! It'll be fun. We'll stay here until the party ends and then get a car uptown."

"Well, I'm not sure—" Gaia glanced over at the door and thought about Jake. Jake, who was probably still within reach, still waiting for the elevator a few feet away.

"You should meet Dad," Chris insisted. "If you're really interested in genetic medicine, you definitely need to talk to him. He can explain this stuff *much* better than I can."

Gaia thought about it. But she didn't have to think very long. She already knew what she wanted to do.

"Sure," she told Chris. "Thanks, I'd love to come."

"Great!" Chris clapped briskly. "We'll have a blast. And *you* all"—he looked down at the Friends of Heather—"can come next time." He flashed them a condescending wink.

"Oh—thanks," Megan said uncertainly. The FOHs were still giving Gaia that wide-eyed look, like she'd been invited to Disneyland and they hadn't.

But Gaia couldn't stop thinking about Jake.

"Excuse me," she said. "I'll be right back."

She pushed open the door, coming back out into

124

the hotel suite's living room, which was still full of music and crowds of shouting kids. Another quarters game had started, and a few people were dancing in the corner. Gaia shoved through the crowds to the suite door and out into the quiet hotel corridor.

"Jake?" she called out. "Jake?"

There was nobody around. The corridor was empty. Gaia walked all the way to the elevators, looking for him, but he was gone.

Somehow the threat was even scarier when it wasn't explained.

all the freaks

"Dear Old" Uncle Oliver

SAM MOON HAD EXHAUSTED ALL HIS options. He'd tried calling Gaia's house at least ten times. He'd even tried going to her apartment on Seventy-second Street, but the doorman had insisted that she wasn't there. No one was there, he'd said. Which somehow didn't surprise Sam, given the nomadic nature of Gaia's life.

But that was fine. Sam was used to not knowing where Gaia was. It went with the territory. Besides, he had a new approach in mind.

He'd tried to talk to Gaia alone about it, but she wouldn't listen or even leave Jake's side for a moment to discuss it. He'd tried talking to Gaia and Jake about it together. No luck there, either. They were too busy being contented lovebirds. So that really left only one other option:

Talking to Jake alone.

It was the only other thing Sam could think of to do. Because one way or another, Sam's point needed to be gotten across. He was not about to let it go. No way. Gaia needed to understand. *Someone* besides Sam needed to understand what was really going on with "dear old" Uncle Oliver.

Sam couldn't get the image out of his head as he walked purposefully down lower Broadway. He kept

127

picturing Oliver, or rather *Loki*, flipping that coin through his fingers again and again during their disturbing little meeting in the park. The look in his eye had been so clear. And so had the bizarrely shifting tone of his voice. Gaia might want very badly to believe that Loki was gone—that there wasn't an ounce of that evil bastard left in her dear sweet uncle, but Sam knew better. He'd seen it with his own eyes. He'd felt it seeping out of Oliver's pores. All the dark and deranged thoughts—all the rage that he was just barely managing to repress. Loki was just biding his time behind that kind facade. He was just waiting for his moment, waiting for the right moment to creep back into Gaia's world and systematically rip it to shreds. Sam didn't know *how* Loki planned to do it or when. He didn't know what exactly Oliver was planning. But he knew it was only a matter of time before they were all suffering again—Gaia, her father, Jake. . . and Sam, too. Sam had never been spared by Loki before; why would this time be any different?

So maybe Jake would listen. Maybe if Sam could talk to him like a man, then Jake would be man enough to listen to reason.

Sam had gotten Jake's number and tried to reach him at home. Jake's father had answered the phone and told Sam that Jake was at his gym, sparring. Sam got the gym's address and was out the door.

Spotting Jake at the gym was incredibly easy. Once

Sam had climbed the stairs to the third floor, passing all the trophies and posters of various karate champions, he had found Jake rather difficult *not* to spot. He was basically devouring his sparring partner in the center mat as various kids in karate uniforms looked on with admiration and envy.

Sam couldn't help but be a little awed himself by Jake's fighting prowess. He was a bit envious, too. But it was an envy of an altogether different kind. He did his best to keep that in check, as it would only get in the way of this very important conversation.

The moment Jake stepped off the mat for some water, Sam moved in.

"Can I talk to you?" Sam asked, trying not to seem like he was sneaking up from behind.

Jake turned around and faced Sam with a look of mild confusion. "What are you doing here?"

"I know," Sam said, nodding. "I know it's a little weird, but I can't find Gaia, and I wanted to talk to you alone anyway."

"Well, you can't find her because she moved. I guess she didn't tell you."

If Sam wasn't mistaken, he could swear Jake was taking a little pleasure in knowing that Gaia hadn't even bothered to inform Sam of her move. But he tried to get past it. He didn't want to have that kind of conversation. That wasn't why he was here. "Moved where?" he asked, as nonchalantly as possible.

"Some kind of boardinghouse on Bank Street. Colling-something. I don't remember. I'll tell her to give you a call." With that Jake turned right around and began to walk away. Things were already a little more tense than Sam had hoped for. But he had to try and stay on good behavior.

"No, wait," Sam said, grabbing Jake's shoulder. Jake turned around and wiped the sweat from his forehead with the towel around his neck. "Can we just—can we talk for just a minute? Please?"

Jake took his sweet time considering it, and then finally he gave a slight nod and led Sam back into the locker room for a little more privacy. He tossed his towel into the bin by the showers and then leaned his back against his locker, giving Sam his somewhat reluctant attention. "What's up?"

Sam leaned against the opposite locker and tried to get to the point as quickly as possible. "Look, I know I've tried this once before with you two, but I was kind of hoping you'd hear me out again. You know... one-on-one."

"About what?"

"About Oliver," Sam said. "You have to understand, Jake. You have to listen to me about this. That man is not right in the head. Loki is still there. He's lurking inside Oliver's head. No, I don't even want to call him Oliver, because that's not who he is. There is no Oliver. He's just Loki with this kind smile pasted over his face, and if we don't—"

"Oh, man," Jake interrupted, "we've heard this stuff, Sam. We've been through this already. You're just off base—you're paranoid. Oliver is an incredible guy. He's, like, a genuine hero. You just don't know what you're talking about."

Sam dropped his head and shook it slowly. Loki had Jake snowed even worse than Sam had thought. That man? The sickest man Sam had ever encountered? A *hero*? God, this was bad. This was really bad.

"No, Jake. Just. . . no." Sam took a deep breath and tried to shake off his frustration. He lifted his head, locked his eyes with Jake's, and tried a different approach. "Look. . . I know that Gaia won't listen to me on this. I know that I'm. . . not the one she listens to anymore." He took a deep breath for his next statement, because it was still a little hard for him to accept. "*You* are, Jake. You are the one she listens to now. And you are the one who needs to protect her. You know that. We both know that's a huge part of being with Gaia: protecting her from all the freaks out there. So that's all I'm asking you to do. I'm asking you to protect her. Protect her from Oliver, Jake. You need to do that; you need to understand it—"

"Hey, Sam," Jake interrupted. He threw his hand out in front of Sam's face, basically telling him to shut up. "Look. . . I really don't want to be an asshole about this, okay? Seriously. But Sam. . . you're right, dude. *I'm* the one who's going to protect her now. Not you.

I'm the one who's going to worry about taking care of her now. Not you. You see my point?"

Sam was feeling more and more deflated by the second. This conversation was going nowhere near where Sam had hoped it would go. And Gaia was no closer to being safe. "This was a bad idea," Sam uttered. "You're not—you don't get it."

"Don't worry about her, Sam. I would never let anything happen to Gaia. Never."

Sam had to accept the fruitless nature of this little visit. But still, he found himself compelled to at least leave Jake with a bit of hard-earned wisdom.

"Don't kid yourself, Jake," he said. "I've made all the mistakes already, and there's one thing I've learned for sure. No one *lets* bad things happen to Gaia. They just happen. And there's not a thing you can do about it. You never know where it's coming from, and you never know who's doing it. Not until it's too late."

"Well, if that's true, then what are you even doing here, Sam?"

"All I said was that there's nothing anyone can really do. That doesn't mean I'm going to stop trying."

Jake finally relaxed his shoulders a bit and nodded. Whether he got the point about Oliver or not, he obviously understood exactly what Sam was talking about.

And with that, Sam turned away and headed for the door. He just had to figure out what the hell he was going to try next.

THE LIMOUSINE SPED NORTH.

Miles of Green Grass

Gaia could barely see out, because the windows were tinted glass. But she knew that they were back in her old neighborhood—the Upper East Side. She could see the tall stone apartment buildings along Fifth Avenue, across from Central Park, as the car smoothly hummed past them.

"I'm so glad you're coming," Chris said. "You're going to love talking to my dad."

"Well, thanks for the invite," Gaia said.

The limousine was slowing down. It pulled up to the curb and stopped. Gaia saw a doorman hurrying over to open the door for them.

She got out first and looked around. It was nearly dark now, a beautiful New York night. The car had stopped on Fifth Avenue in front of a big, old-fashioned apartment building with a dark red awning. Looking up, she could see balconies stretching around the building's upper floors, facing Central Park.

Liz and Chris hopped out of the limousine as if they'd been doing it all their lives—which, Gaia figured, they probably had. "Hi, Marko," Chris said to the doorman. "Nice haircut."

"Thank you, Mr. Rodke. Ms. Rodke." The doorman

133

nodded smoothly at them and then hurried ahead to open the building's front door.

"You'll have to forgive the apartment," Liz told Gaia apologetically as they stood in the rising elevator. The elevator's interior was polished mahogany. Chris had punched the button for the seventeenth floor, Gaia saw. "We've only been here like a week; there's still construction going on."

"I wouldn't worry about it," Gaia joked. There was most definitely nothing to be ashamed of in this ridiculous building. The elevator arrived on seventeen, and the wide metal doors slid open.

Gaia went first. She stepped out into a small vestibule covered with striped wallpaper. As she walked forward, a big black apartment door swung open. A slim, elegantly dressed middle-aged woman stood there, smiling. She wore large gold earrings and a Chanel jacket. It was obvious from her face that she was Liz and Chris's mother.

"You must be Gaia," Mrs. Rodke said, extending her hand. "How do you do—I'm Blair Rodke."

"Hi," Gaia said, wondering if there was some whole batch of etiquette here that she knew nothing about. But Mrs. Rodke smiled warmly, so she figured she hadn't done anything wrong yet.

"Hi, Mom," Liz said, leaning to kiss Mrs. Rodke's cheek.

Gaia had been in some fairly fancy places in her life.

But there'd been nothing in her experience quite like the Rodke apartment. The word *apartment* didn't really convey what it was like—the place was more like a mansion that had been lifted seventeen stories off the ground and placed atop a Manhattan apartment tower.

"Are we eating soon?" Chris asked his mother. "I'm starving."

"Sure—not too long now," Mrs. Rodke said. "Just a few minutes. Gaia, can I get you anything?"

"Oh, no, thanks," Gaia said, fixating on the huge windows.

They were in an extremely spacious entryway with a marble floor. A glass table in the middle of the room held a shallow bowl of water with lilies floating in it. The ceiling was high and dark. A big curved staircase stood to one side, leading up to another corridor on the floor above. Spotlit paintings hung on the walls. A stack of plywood against one wall showed that the place was still under construction.

Liz and Chris led the way forward. Gaia followed them around a corner into a living room that was the size of a school gym. At least that was how it looked to Gaia. Maybe the room looked bigger because it contained almost no furniture at all. One entire wall was glass, facing a tiled balcony overlooking the park. Gaia found herself walking toward it without thinking.

Chris and Liz walked up next to her, and they stood side by side, leaning on the balcony's stone parapet, gazing down at the park. It was an incredible view. The sun was just setting, and the towers of Central Park West shone against the sky across the park. There were miles of grass and trees seventeen stories down, and Gaia could almost smell the fragrant aroma of the greenery far below.

"This is just awesome," Liz said. It was true. "I hope I never take this for granted."

"It's beautiful," Gaia said.

Standing there between the Rodkes, Gaia thought for a moment about how much her life had changed. And so quickly—D., her newfound brother; Jake; Oliver. . . the boardinghouse. . . the sudden new attitudes from the FOHs. . . the Rodkes. . . Jake. Maybe Chris was right. Maybe a person really could change.

How many fights? Gaia wondered, gazing down at the park. *Right down there? How many ass kickings? And what for? What does all that mean?*

"Hello, kids." A male voice came from behind them.

Gaia turned around. A handsome, middle-aged man stood in the open balcony door. He wore a blue denim shirt and jeans. His chestnut hair blew around his kind, square face with its faint wrinkles and crow's-feet. The man was holding a drink and smiling pleasantly at Gaia. He had piercing blue eyes, just like his son.

"You must be Gaia," the man said, stepping forward and extending his hand. "Robert Rodke."

136

"Hi," Gaia said, shaking hands. It was so immediately obvious that he was a man of substance. Intelligent and accomplished and, most of all, real.

"Shall we go in?" Mr. Rodke suggested.

He led them into the dining room. The floor was covered by a white drop cloth; Gaia saw that the ceiling was half unpainted. But the rest of the room was breathtaking. An enormous oak table filled the center of the room. Blair Rodke was waiting with a drink as a pair of uniformed maids finished setting the table. A place had been laid for Gaia.

"Gaia, you'll have to tell us all about New York," Mrs. Rodke said. "We've got a lot to learn. Have you lived here all your life?"

"No, but I guess I feel like I have now."

"Oh, and Chris tells me you're interested in *genetics,* Gaia," Mr. Rodke said. "A young lady after my own heart. Is that true?"

"Well—" Gaia was taken aback. "I'm not an expert or anything. Just. . . you know. . . interested." The understatement of the century.

"Yeah," Chris said. "We were talking a little earlier about making changes, you know, things you can and can't change. I told her there's nothing today that you can't change."

"Can we not get into this again?" Liz complained. "Mom, can you stop him? I've been listening to this all afternoon—"

"Well, I mean, your genes determine who you are," Gaia said. "It's natural—there's no escaping that."

"Oh, untrue, Gaia," Mr. Rodke said. "Gaia, what do you think modern science is *for*?"

"Dad, no speech," Liz moaned. "Please, no speech. Now you'll see where Chris gets it from, Gaia."

"I'll keep it short," Mr. Rodke laughed. "I say science is about removing natural boundaries. People can't fly, right? But with airplanes they can. We can't breathe underwater or in space—but technology lets us go there anyway. Genes are the next frontier. The next opportunity for improving people's lives."

The maids were placing fragrant plates in front of everyone—Gaia noticed that they started with Mrs. Rodke and then moved on to Liz and herself before serving the men. It was all very proper. Looking down, Gaia saw that she had three forks and two knives.

"The next—what do you mean, improving people's lives?" Gaia asked.

Maybe things are changing, she thought wildly. *Really changing. Maybe I don't know as much as I think I do.*

"You seem very interested in this," Mr. Rodke said. "If it's not too intrusive a question, may I ask why?"

"Well, I—" Gaia had no idea what to say. It was precisely the question she didn't want to answer.

"Because she's *smart*, Dad," Chris said easily. He was cutting enthusiastically into his lamb.

"Gaia, if you're really interested, you should come

down to the office. I'd be happy to show you all the things we're doing."

"I'd love that," Gaia blurted.

Immediately she regretted having spoken. It was rude and overeager, but she couldn't help it.

"If you'd like, I could probably even find time for you tomorrow. How would that be?"

Gaia smiled. "That would be great," she said. "That would be just. . . perfect. Thank you, Mr. Rodke. Seriously."

Rodke waved a dismissive hand. "Please don't mention it," he said, smiling back. "I believe in educating future generations. You might play a major role in the history of genetics someday."

I might, Gaia thought. *I just might.*

GAIA WAS STANDING ON SIXTH AVENUE,

Screwed-up DNA

watching a flood of businesspeople flying in and out of the revolving doors of a sixty-story green glass building. The two-foot-high polished chrome sign read Rodke and Simon. It had to be lunchtime; the building's twin granite fountains were swamped by crowds of suited men and women seated along their edges, eating sandwiches out of paper deli wrappers.

Secretaries, executives, and delivery guys were all threading their way past each other in a sort of intricate, choreographed ballet, hefting their briefcases and yelling into their cell phones.

Is this really what I want to be doing? Gaia asked herself, walking toward the Rodke and Simon entranceway. She wasn't sure what the answer was, but she'd already come all the way up here—and she couldn't exactly stand Mr. Rodke up. It would look bad, and it might even cause friction with Liz and Chris.

She pulled open the heavy chrome-and-glass door and went in.

Enter Gaia Moore, serious young biology student.

It seemed plausible, Gaia thought as the blast of air-conditioning hit her. She could be a science geek. Mr. Rodke already saw her that way—that was why she was here.

Gaia felt very self-conscious in the elevator. She was packed in with a crowd of Attractive Young Businesspeople, all of whom wore very expensive looking suits and gleaming shoes and wristwatches. Her ears popped as the elevator shot upward, bonging gently as it stopped on the forty-first floor.

The air up here was even colder. Gaia stepped off the elevator, her scuffed sneakers leaving tracks in the flawless beige carpeting. She was in a vast entryway, with another gigantic chrome Rodke and Simon logo on the wall. A row of modern white padded chairs faced a dark rectangular screen set into the fabric-covered wall. There didn't seem to be anyone else around.

The elevator door slid shut behind her. Gaia stepped forward, clutching her book bag. Now she could see a beige desk to one side with yet another Rodke and Simon logo set into it. A severe-looking young woman in tortoiseshell glasses and a prim suit sat there, wearing a headset, staring at a computer monitor and typing.

"Excuse me," Gaia said. "Um—"

The woman looked up at her and then beamed. "Gaia Moore?"

"Yes—"

"How do you do. I'm Emily Baskin." The woman stood up. She was still smiling brightly at Gaia. She put out her hand. "Public affairs associate for Rodke and Simon. If you would please take a seat, Mr. Rodke will be with you in just one moment."

"Um—okay, thanks," Gaia said, shaking hands.

"Here," Emily Baskin said, handing over a big glossy folder. "You can look at this while you wait."

Gaia went over to the row of white seats, looking at the folder. *Rodke and Simon: Building a Global Future,* the cover read. There was a picture of a man in a white lab coat holding a beaker of amber fluid.

141

Gaia sat down on one of the plush white chairs. The moment she did so, the dark rectangular screen in front of her came to life. Music started playing as an animated version of the Rodke and Simon logo appeared on the screen. Behind the logo a series of photographs faded in and out, showing containers of shampoo, toothpaste, prescription drugs, suntan lotion, lipstick—every kind of product you could buy at a drugstore.

"Welcome to Rodke and Simon," a deep-voiced male narrator said. "Building a global future."

Now the screen was showing cities around the world and white-coated scientists working in laboratories.

"Rodke and Simon is the world industry leader in cosmetic and pharmaceutical technology," the narrator went on. He sounded like a judge or a cop: the world's most authoritative voice. "With assets in excess of two hundred billion dollars, Rodke and Simon has offices and laboratories in twelve major cities around the globe and holds forty-two separate chemical patents. Since 1972 Rodke and Simon has stood for—"

"Gaia!"

She turned her head. Mr. Rodke was walking toward her, his hand already out. He was wearing a suit that must have cost four thousand dollars.

"Hello, Mr. Rodke," she said awkwardly, getting up off the couch.

"Please, call me Robert," he said, smiling easily. His

handshake was firm and quick. "I'm so sorry to keep you waiting. Emily, turn that off, would you?"

"Yes, Mr. Rodke," Emily said quickly. She pressed a button on her desk and the promotional film suddenly stopped, cutting the world's most authoritative voice off in midsentence.

"Did you get a brochure?" Rodke asked, looking over at Gaia. "Good. Let's go somewhere more comfortable, shall we? Have you had lunch?"

"What? Oh—yes," Gaia said. She was hurrying to keep up with Rodke as he held a wide oak door open for her and then strode forward along a bright, carpeted corridor. Giant plate-glass windows showed a dazzling view of Midtown Manhattan, its towers and spires sparkling in the bright midday sun. "Thanks so much for taking the time to see me."

Rodke frowned, waving a hand dismissively. "Not at all. We're all about the future here at R&S: you may have noticed our slogan. I've always got time for a young scientist like yourself."

Gaia felt a twinge of guilt at that. This man was going out of his way for her based on a false pretense. *I'm not a scientist. I can still tell him that, tell him why I'm really here.*

"This way," Rodke said, gesturing toward a massive double oak door. "Marion, no calls," he barked out at a young blond woman seated at a desk nearby.

"Yes, Mr. Rodke," the woman said briskly.

Gaia had never seen such a large office in her life. It was nearly the size of the cafeteria at the Village School. A gigantic oak desk stood near massive floor-to-ceiling windows. Bright sunlight was blasting into the office. Out the window Gaia could see the Hudson River twinkling in the sun like pebbled glass far in the distance. To one side, a ten-foot-tall chrome sculpture of a DNA molecule stood on a green granite base. Two couches flanked a glass coffee table, which held a stack of the same glossy brochures Gaia had been given.

"Please, take a seat," Rodke said, gesturing toward a leather chair. "And let's talk about genetics."

Gaia sat down. She realized she was excited—Rodke's brisk manner was contagious. There was something about the way he spoke that appealed to her: direct and serious.

"Last night," Gaia said, "you were talking about improving people's lives."

"Through knowledge," Rodke said, dropping into a massive chair behind his equally massive desk. "Through learning. You know, a hundred years ago they didn't even know what DNA *was*?" Rodke squinted fervently. "They knew something was happening when they bred horses, but the science was a mystery. Today there's no mystery at all—we breed for speed, for strength, for anything you want. Now, thanks to science, we can *change* traits. What do you want to be, Gaia? Taller? Shorter? Brunette? Green eyed?" Rodke pointed at Gaia. The afternoon sun backlit his thick hair. "Smarter? Faster? All traits that used to be set in stone from birth, and almost all of them can be changed."

"But you're talking about two different things," Gaia said. "You can change the results of someone's genes—give a bald man back his hair or dye someone's hair—but you can't change the genes *themselves*."

Rodke smiled. "Who says we can't? Gaia, you should *see* what we're doing here. We are beginning to do exactly what you just said—change the genes directly. Alter a person's genetic pattern so that everything that used to be determined in that person's life can now be changed."

Gaia couldn't believe what she was hearing. All the attention she paid to the CIA and the Organization and her family problems and fighting and Jake and all of it, and she had never truly focused her attention on the core problem of her life—her genetic code. She hadn't ever focused on it because there was nothing she could do about it.

Except maybe there *was*.

She wasn't about to start talking to Robert Rodke about her own screwed-up DNA. That was out of the question.

But she had to learn more about what Rodke and Simon was doing. She *had* to.

"Can you tell me more about what you're doing?"

"Only in a limited way," Rodke said apologetically. "I certainly can't master the technical details. I'm just a lowly CEO. If you're really interested, you should talk to Dr. Ulrich. He's working on all kinds of genetic alteration techniques. He can explain much better than I can."

"Dr. Ulrich?" Gaia wondered if she was supposed to recognize the name.

"He's our resequencing guru. Gaia, I've managed to drag a *very* well known and very expensive geneticist away from Princeton University. He works for me now in our new lab right here in this building. Would you like to meet him?"

"Well—"

Genetic alteration techniques, Gaia thought. The phrase was incredibly suggestive.

Gaia was surprised at how quickly this was moving. Maybe *too* quickly. At a certain point all these terribly nice people were going to want to know *why* she was so interested in what they were doing.

Still, what could it hurt to talk to a scientist? His time couldn't be more valuable than a CEO's.

"Sure," Gaia said, brushing her unkempt hair back from her face. "That would be great."

Rodke was reaching for the phone. "Let me call him right now," he said. "Karl's a busy man—he's barely got time for *me*. But I'm sure he'd be interested in meeting a bright, young American student of genetics."

Or a girl born without the fear gene, Gaia thought.
If I could find a way to keep that a secret.

"NINE P.M.," THE SPEAKING CLOCK

Hate Each Other

said.

Heather could barely hear it. She was three doors away in the small, windowless room reserved for phone conversations. One of the special Braille phones was in front of her on a table.

The room was empty except for Heather. She could tell, from the feel of the air and the silence.

Here goes, she thought.

Heather's heart was beating fast. It had only been a day since those two men—Rowan and Morrow—had visited her room and asked her those strange questions, but she was still frightened. She had barely slept a wink that night.

Heather picked up the phone receiver. Its plastic surface felt cold and slick.

Don't tell anybody *about us,* Rowan had told her. He'd stood right in front of her and put his hand on her shoulder and threatened her directly. *If you do, we'll find out. And we'll come back. Do you understand?*

147

Heather understood. Somehow the threat was even scarier when it wasn't explained. And she'd agreed in her mind. She would keep her mouth shut. At least, that was what she'd thought right then, at that moment.

Heather reached for the keypad. Her fingers brushed the Braille buttons, and she started dialing. It was easy to tell which button was which; she'd gotten good at it.

One. Two one two. Five five five. Twelve twelve.

New York City directory assistance.

A day later Heather's feelings had changed a bit. She was still frightened, but now she was angry, too. Heather didn't know much about government bureaucrats, but she was pretty sure they didn't threaten people. So if Rowan and Morrow weren't bureaucrats, who the hell were they?

"Residence of Gaia Moore," Heather told the recording. "East Seventy-second Street in Manhattan."

She had to warn Gaia. It was that simple; she had no choice. How could those men "find out," anyway? Heather didn't think they could. That was just something they'd said to scare her. It was obvious now.

And all their questions had been about Gaia.

There was a click as Heather was connected to a live operator. She got ready to memorize the number—something else she'd gotten good at.

"That number is no longer in service," the operator told her.

Heather hung up. A cold wave passed over her.

Could they have gotten to her? So fast? A day later?

Heather told herself that was silly. It had been a long time since she'd been in New York. It had been a while since she'd spoken to Gaia or anyone else. She'd moved, that was all. Heather had to warn someone else—get the message to Gaia.

One. Two one two...

Heather's fingers pressed the Braille buttons. The phone receiver, next to her ear, was already damp with her perspiration. This number she knew all too well.

The phone was ringing. It picked up. Immediately she heard music in the background and shuffling noises.

"Hello?"

Ed's voice. Unmistakably. Heather felt a wave of relief at the sound of Ed's voice.

"Ed, it's Heather."

"Heather?" Ed sounded a bit stunned but pleased. "Wow. I don't believe—how are you?"

"Fine. Okay. Not so good."

"What's wrong?"

Don't tell anyone, Rowan had warned her.

Too bad.

"Ed, listen," Heather said. "You have to do something for me."

"Sure," Ed said affably. "Anything. Name it."

"You have to give a message to Gaia."

"That's going to be difficult," Ed said heavily.

149

There was silence at the other end of the phone. Heather could hear Ed breathing in and out.

"Why?" Heather croaked. "Why will it be difficult?"

"We're, um—we're not exactly speaking."

"Not—" Heather was relieved. *She's all right,* she thought. *Relax.*

But wait. Ed and Gaia? Not *speaking*? That was crazy. What could possibly have driven a wedge like that between Gaia and Ed? Heather was almost afraid to ask. "Ed, what happened?"

"That's a long story. She—it's really the best thing for both of us right now. And there's—" Ed paused again, and Heather realized, with her newfound ability to read voices and detect moods, that this was something recent that Ed was reacting to. "There's someone else in the picture. She's got a—Gaia's been spending a lot of time with a guy named Jake."

Jake? Heather didn't have the slightest idea who that was. It reminded her again how long she'd been away from New York.

"Do you think you could talk to her anyway?" Heather went on. "I'm sorry, Ed, but it's important. Can you just tell her that I think she might be in some kind of trouble?"

"What?"

"Two men came here yesterday. And. . . they were kind of scary. They asked me a whole bunch of questions about what happened to me, about being blind. . .

150

and about Gaia. They were seriously kind of scary, Ed. And I'm afraid they're going to come looking for her."

"Of course." Ed laughed bitterly. "Someone is always looking for Gaia."

"They told me not to tell anyone," Heather went on. "But I had to, Ed."

"Right." Ed was breathing again. "What did they look—oh, sorry."

"I can't tell you what they looked like. They talked about Oliver, too—you know, Gaia's uncle. Could you just tell her what happened? Please, Ed?"

He's not going to do it, Heather thought. *They hate each other now, and he's not going to talk to her.*

"Nine-ten P.M.," the speaking clock in the next room said.

"Of course," Ed said quickly. Heather's concern melted away. "Of course I'll do it."

"You don't mind?"

"No, I don't. . . . I mean, we're not really talk—no, forget that. Forget it. If you think she's in trouble. . . then I don't have a choice."

"Good." Heather felt a wave of admiration for Ed. She could tell from the weariness in his voice how much he didn't want to do it. But he was going to come through as usual.

"Let me make sure I've got the story straight," Ed said. All traces of resentment were gone from his voice. "Two men came to harass you and asked questions about your blindness; they mentioned her uncle and gave the impression that they're going to talk to her next. Do I have it right?"

A wave of relief passed over Heather; it was almost a physical feeling of a weight being lifted. *I've done the right thing,* she thought firmly. She was sure of it.

"Yeah, you got it right. Thanks, Ed. Thanks so much."

"That's okay."

"I miss you, Ed." It was true. She missed everybody. She could spend the next ten minutes giving Ed greetings to pass on to everyone. But that could wait. "Please, just talk to Gaia as soon as you can. It's important."

"All right," Ed said. "I'll do it. Don't worry."

"Thanks, Ed." Heather suddenly felt like crying, she missed everyone so much.

That's done, Heather thought, hanging up the phone. *And there's no way those two men will find out.*

But she wasn't sure. And she was mildly surprised to find that she was still as frightened as before.

All she could do was **easy** sit there like a **answers** tortured zombie.

WHAT AM I DOING HERE?

Gaia wasn't sure. She was back in the Rodke and Simon building on Sixth Avenue. She was shivering—the waiting room's air-conditioning was going full

Immeasurably Grateful

blast. Pleasant music was playing quietly in the background. Gaia sat in one of the comfortable leather chairs, holding her package in her lap, looking around.

The room was empty except for the white-coated receptionist behind the desk. The receptionist had smiled at her and told her to wait (in a British accent) and then ignored her. Every time the phone rang, the receptionist answered quietly, "Rodke and Simon, Advanced Resequencing Labs."

When Mr. Rodke had arranged this meeting from his office, he'd told her to expect a bit of a "madhouse" since the laboratories were so new. Gaia wouldn't have called this a "madhouse," however. Like the Rodkes' apartment, the office had stacks of plywood and construction materials around, but each person she'd seen—the receptionist and the passing scientists in lab coats—had appeared very calm and professional. The atmosphere of high-end science was unmistakable.

So why am I here?

It was a funny series of events, now that she thought

back on it. If she hadn't played chess in Starbucks. . . if she hadn't gotten an opportunity to meet Mr. Rodke. . . if he hadn't graciously invited her to come find out about his company. . . she wouldn't be sitting here, with this package in her lap, about to have a private discussion with one of the world's premier geneticists.

Gaia was rehearsing the things she was going to say. In her fingers the package turned over and over. She could still leave, she thought, turn right around and take the elevator down to Sixth Avenue and get a subway home to Collingwood. She'd tell Mr. Rodke that she'd changed her mind.

But she *hadn't* changed her mind. She wanted to be here. It was as simple as that. *I'm just learning,* she told herself. *The more knowledge I have, the better off I am.*

"Miss Moore?" the receptionist said. Again her British accent struck Gaia. It made her sound so reasonable, so professional. "Dr. Ulrich will see you now."

"Thank you," Gaia said. Clutching her small paper-wrapped package, she rose to her feet and followed the receptionist's gesture toward a white metal door.

Resequencing Analysis Systems, a sign on the door said. And beneath that, in smaller letters, Karl Ulrich. No alphabet soup of initials and credentials; just his name. Gaia found that reassuring somehow.

She noticed that the door had a complicated electronic combination lock. The lock wasn't engaged—she could push the door open.

The room inside was much colder and much larger. Gaia's breath was actually fogging before her face. There were no windows. The room was dominated by a large Formica-covered table about the size of four Ping-Pong tables pushed together. It was covered in stacks of round petri dishes, piled up like transparent hockey pucks.

At one end of the table was a large gray machine like a bank safe. The machine had a complicated computer connection coming off it and a big round door on its front, like a washing machine. The interior of the machine was brightly lit.

"You must be Gaia Moore," Dr. Ulrich said, coming toward her. He was a short, dark-haired man with a heavy German accent. He had thick gold-framed glasses. He wore a white lab coat and latex surgical gloves; he was pulling off the gloves to shake hands. "How do you do? Sorry about the cold air—it is necessary for the tissue samples."

"Hello," Gaia said. She was still clutching her small `paper-wrapped package`.

Dr. Ulrich gestured to one side, where a metal desk stood against the wall. Stacks of papers and more petri dishes covered its surface. There was a chair facing the desk, and Gaia sat down. "This place is pretty amazing," Gaia said, doing her best to make conversation.

"Well, yes, but we have a lot of work still to do," Ulrich said. His accent was pronounced; *have* sounded like *haff*. Grunting, Dr. Ulrich dropped into a battered leather chair behind his desk. "This new facility is very exciting. Mr. Rodke has come through on his promises to provide the best of everything. Our work is going very well, mostly thanks to *that*."

Ulrich was pointing at the big bank safe–looking machine. Gaia looked over politely. "And what's that?"

Ulrich waved a hand dismissively. "Much too complicated. If I answered your question, we would be talking for three hours."

"But I'm interested," Gaia protested.

"Ah, yes, I forget—you are a student of the human genome." Ulrich beamed at her, his glasses glinting in the fluorescent light. "Robert Rodke told me as much. So—that machine is our pride and joy. It is an advanced electron microscope specially configured to allow a complete examination of any chromosome from any tissue sample. It is connected to very powerful computers in the basement of this building.

"Simply put, with this device we can now determine the genetic properties of any living organism and so probe the mysteries of heredity. It takes mere moments. It is no exaggeration to call this the most advanced gene sequencer on the planet. For this machine alone, the company has spent close to two hundred million dollars."

Gaia kept looking at the machine. It looked so normal, so boring.

But that could be the key, she realized. *The key to my whole life.* That machine could look at her blood and see what made her fearless.

"But you can't *change* people's genes with that thing, can you?" Gaia asked.

Ulrich leaned forward, intently nodding. "Just so. We cannot do this here. To alter genes, a much more complex procedure is involved over at the hospital, where we have set up our new facility. But again, I talk too much about details."

"It's interesting," said Gaia truthfully.

Our new facility. . . over at the hospital. It was clear that these people meant business. The whole thing seemed very serious and professional. Gaia was impressed, and, more importantly, she was realizing again how lucky she was. Lucky that she'd met the Rodke kids. Lucky that they liked her. Lucky that they'd started talking about genes. And now here she was, sitting in the same room with the most advanced gene sequencer on the planet.

"So what are we to discuss?" Ulrich asked politely. He had taken off his glasses and was polishing them with a white cloth. His face was craggy and kind; his eyes were dark brown. "I understand that you have some questions for me."

"Yeah," Gaia said. She had spent some time planning this the night before; she knew exactly what she wanted to say. "Dr. Ulrich, can I make a deal with you?

Can we agree that this conversation is private? Strictly between us?"

Ulrich frowned. His glasses glinted as he put them back on. "Of course. You must understand that this goes both ways: when you leave this room, you must be careful not to give away any of the company's valuable trade secrets regarding techniques that are not yet available to the general public."

Gaia was unwrapping her package.

"I know a person," she explained, "who has a. . . disease. I guess you could call it a disease. There's something. . . unusual about this person."

"Go on."

"There's a family history of disorder," Gaia went on. She was choosing her words carefully. "There's a direct genetic cause for all of it. This person's uncle had a rare blood disease in childhood, and there's a younger sibling with very unusual psychological traits. But the point is, this person might want to be. . . cured of the disease if it's possible."

"I would not know how to discuss this," Ulrich said. "I do not know the details."

"Look," Gaia said.

She'd opened her package and brought out a very small glass bottle the size of a thimble. The bottle was tightly sealed, and sliding around inside were a few drops of dark red fluid.

Human blood.

When Ulrich saw the bottle, his eyes widened. He leaned forward, peering at the object in Gaia's hand.

"The person I'm discussing is very concerned about privacy," Gaia went on. "But the possibility that the. . . disease. . . could be treated is very attractive to this person. So the person agreed to give me a blood sample for you to examine."

"Just so. Please, let me see?"

Ulrich's hand reached toward her across the desk. Gaia handed over the bottle—the bottle she'd stolen from the Village School's science lab and filled with `her own blood` that morning in the bathroom at the Collingwood boardinghouse.

"Arterial blood; drawn in the last six hours, judging by the color and coagulation. Come this way," Ulrich said, quickly snapping a new pair of white surgical gloves onto his hands. "Let us see what you have."

Here goes, Gaia thought as she followed the small man across the room toward the big table and the hulking gray machine. *Now we'll see if this guy's as good as he thinks he is.*

Gaia watched as Dr. Ulrich's gloved hands quickly transferred her blood onto a small metal grille the size of a quarter. He moved very fast. First he used tweezers to put the blood-soaked metal disk into a steel bottle shaped like a soup can. Next he screwed its cover down tight, creating a vacuum seal. Then he swung open the big round door on his machine. Inside, the walls were copper mesh. He carefully placed the steel bottle in the center of the machine's cavity and then closed the door and latched it tightly shut. Unexpectedly, he then reached for a telephone on the table and dialed.

"Donaldson?" Ulrich said into the phone. "*Ja*, it's me. Could you please start a sequence now? The chamber is loaded."

As Gaia watched, the machine suddenly started clanking and humming all by itself. A brilliant light shone out of its round window; Gaia's eyes watered and she had to look away.

"This will now take just a few moments," Ulrich said, leading Gaia back to his desk. Behind them the machine kept humming and clicking. "The computer lab is downstairs; this is where they control the genetic examination. We will see the results here."

"Okay," Gaia said. She resumed her seat as before, facing Ulrich across the desk. "That's pretty amazing, that it works so fast."

"Amazing, yes. But we have paid for that speed with years and years of testing. The technique is only just now becoming feasible; a few months ago it would not have been possible to get the results so quickly. If all goes well, soon every hospital will have one of these. Then the treatment of—ah!"

A laser printer on the floor was making clicking

noises as pieces of paper slid out. Dr. Ulrich reached down and picked them up. He began reading.

Then he frowned.

Gaia glanced back over at the two-hundred-million-dollar machine. It was silent now. Its lights had gone out.

The phone rang. Ulrich picked it up; he was still squinting at the pages. "Hello? *Ja,* I see it, too. And the missing portions. . . are you sure this is not another software problem?"

There was a pause, during which Gaia could hear a man's voice speaking loudly on the other end of the phone.

"Of course I loaded the machine correctly," Ulrich said angrily. "What do you take me for, a fool? But you are correct: it cannot possibly be faked. . . . Well, if you are sure, then I am sure."

Ulrich slammed down the phone. "That was the computer lab—they can be troublesome," he told Gaia. "This is perhaps the most extraordinary human chromosome I have ever seen, Ms. Moore. A person with these genes. . ." The man shook his head, as if lost in thought. "Well, the results would be remarkable. There is no way of telling how a person would exist without. . ."

He can see it, Gaia thought. *He can actually see it.*

"Remember," Gaia said, "that you promised to keep this a secret."

"Hmmm?" Ulrich looked at her sharply, as if suddenly remembering that he wasn't alone in the room. "Oh, yes—of course. But you must understand, Ms.

Moore, this person whose blood you have shown me—this 'disease,' as you call it—is unique in my experience. Such a person could be exhibited in scientific conferences around the world for years, if it were permissible."

"But you could treat it?" Gaia asked, leaning forward in her chair. Her breath was fogging in front of her face; the coldness of the room was getting to her. "If the person came to you. . . you could fix the person's genes? Make them normal?"

Ulrich stared back at Gaia. He was reaching into his breast pocket. He pulled out a business card and handed it over. He was still wearing his surgical gloves.

Gaia looked down at the card. It had Ulrich's name, a Rodke and Simon logo, and, penciled in underneath, another phone number and address.

"It is as if you had read my mind," Ulrich said intently. "That is precisely what I would be most interested in doing. The successful completion of such a procedure would be a tremendous scientific breakthrough. It would bring me and my colleagues immeasurably closer to our goals. I simply never dreamed that such a person. . . that such a unique genome. . . could naturally occur. By correcting nature's 'mistake,' I could take a quantum leap in understanding blood-related diseases and imbalances. So, yes, Gaia," the doctor concluded. "I would be quite willing to do what you say."

"I see." Gaia tried to appear calm, but she wanted to scream with excitement.

"I understand that you are interested in confidentiality," Ulrich went on, "so I give you my home number. If the person you speak of wishes to discuss this condition and how to treat it, he or she may contact me in confidence. But as I have said, I would be immeasurably grateful for an opportunity to study this incredible chromosome in more detail, even as its effects were corrected and removed."

Corrected and removed, Gaia thought. She almost felt dizzy. Those two words contained the magic formula for changing her entire life.

"Okay," Gaia said, taking a deep breath. She rose to her feet. "Okay. Thanks, Dr. Ulrich. Thanks for taking the time to see me."

"No, thank *you,*" Ulrich said sincerely, reaching to shake hands. "You are a most interesting young lady. And you have brought me priceless blood."

THE MORE SHE THOUGHT ABOUT IT,

the lonelier she felt: her big fat secret, her big fat genetic glitch and all its pros and cons and ups and downs and joys and pains— Gaia had run her options through her head so many times that they

Tortured Zombie

had grown ragged and stale and downright unbearable. But she just couldn't focus on anything else. Certainly not school.

So here she was, sitting on the hot stone stoop of a brownstone, staring at the dark weathered doors of the Village School with her mind in a horrible mess of impenetrable knots. She might as well have had a forty in one hand and a cigarette in the other, like every other pathetic squatter in the village. All she could do was sit there like a `tortured zombie,` cutting class for no reason at all, like the most clichéd juvenile delinquent in New York.

The real agony was the not talking, trying to carry on the entire dialectic in her own head. But she couldn't talk about it. Who was she going to talk to? Oliver? She was thrilled to have the real Oliver back in her life, but they hadn't reached *that* level of trust just yet. Besides, it would just be too weird looking into the face that once belonged to Loki and trying to talk about this. Way too much nightmare flashback potential. Jake? She was already avoiding Jake in her own inimitably pathetic style. She wasn't even ready to have the whole commitment conversation, let alone try to figure out how to broach this monster subject. No, there was no one. The subject was simply undiscussable.

Unfortunately, it looked like Chris Rodke was going to try to discuss it anyway.

Chris pushed through the old school doors and immediately spotted Gaia across the street.

Keep walking, she begged silently. *Please, Chris. Just keep walking.*

But it was no use. Before she could even open her mouth to say no, Chris had jogged the few steps across the street and sat himself down right next to her on the stoop. The look on his face was so damn kind, she almost felt guilty for wishing so very much that he would just leave her alone.

It wasn't that she didn't like Chris. She did. She liked his intelligence and his straightforwardness and his brotherly ease. She'd found an unexpectedly high comfort level with Chris and Liz, and that was no small feat in the social life of Gaia Moore. But on this particular day, at this particular hour, she really just wanted to sit with her irreconcilable thoughts and stew in a pool of old-Gaia futility. Chris wouldn't allow it.

"All right, look," he said, leaning forward and bumping his shoulder against Gaia's. "I have no idea what it is that's put that dreadful look on your face. But I know you're going to burst a blood vessel in your brain if you don't talk about it."

"I'm fine," Gaia mumbled. She had too much respect for Chris to give him her patented "piss off" stare. "Really, I'm fine. It's just. . . a mood."

"Uh-huh." He smiled dubiously. "Right. A mood. You're a bad liar, Gaia, did anyone ever tell you that?"

"It's not my forte," she admitted, keeping her eyes fixed straight ahead.

"Hey. . ." He leaned his face closer to hers and bumped her shoulder even harder. "*Hey.*"

Gaia finally turned toward him. Anything to avoid another shoulder bump. "What?"

Chris pulled off his shades, revealing his inhumanly blue eyes. "Look," he sighed, "I know we're not exactly best buddies just yet. But in my personal opinion, if you've got a problem—if you're mulling something over right now—it's actually far better to discuss it with someone you *don't* know so well. Objective advice is what you need." Chris suddenly thrust his hand out for a handshake. "Chris Rodke." He grinned. "Teen psychiatrist. I specialize in pain, confusion, and unbearable existential angst."

"Chris," she said as gently as she could, "I really don't want to talk about it."

"Yes, you do," he insisted.

"No. . . I really don't."

"Um. . . yes. You really do. Try me, Gaia. You won't be disappointed. Ask Liz. I'm good at this stuff. Tell me what's going on in that fashionably disheveled head of yours."

"Okay, look," she said, running her hands through her hair self-consciously. "What is the nicest, most respectful, most inoffensive way for me to get you to leave me alone?"

It was risky, but its only effect was to widen Chris's grin. No matter what she did, it only seemed to make

Chris like her more. Which she supposed was a good thing.

"Easy," he said. "Tell me what's up. You tell me what your problem is, I give you some A-1 golden advice. Your problem is instantly solved. And then I leave." Chris threw his hands out and smiled with Tom Cruisian confidence.

"Right," she said with a snort. "Sure." She dropped her head in her hands and pressed her palms firmly against her eyes. "*Ugh*. Chris, my life is torture. You have no idea. My life is nothing other than the repeated application of cruel sadistic torture, over and over and over and over—"

"Hi," Chris interrupted her suddenly.

"Hi?" What does he mean, "Hi"?

Gaia brought her head back up toward him and quickly realized that he was talking to someone else. She followed Chris's sight line to her left, and then her lungs instantly compressed to the point of near suffocation. Standing only inches from her shoulder, right next to the stoop, was none other than Ed Fargo.

Gaia was at a loss. Being at this close proximity to Ed was so unusual that it had left her momentarily speechless. Avoidance and distance. Those were supposed to be the rules. Not that Gaia exactly delighted in those rules, but that was how Ed had wanted it, wasn't it? So what was he doing here, breaking the rules?

Ed seemed to be somewhat vocally challenged

himself. The silence between them was getting louder and louder.

Chris broke it first. "Um. . . I'm Chris," he said, obviously feeling compelled to break the world's most awkward silence.

"I know," Ed said, leaving Gaia's eyes momentarily to shake hands with Chris. "Ed."

"Well, Ed, maybe you can help me out. I'm trying to cheer up my friend Gaia here, but she's what we call 'help rejecting.'" Chris made quotation marks with his fingers.

Ed turned back to Gaia. "What's wrong?" The instant concern in his eyes made Gaia suddenly want to cry, though she had no idea why.

"Nothing," she said quietly. "Don't mind him." She gestured to Chris. "He's just trying to be a pain in my ass."

Another awkward silence followed.

"Um. . . can I talk to you?" Ed finally asked.

Gaia had no clue what to make of such a question. She only knew that it kept her heart stuck somewhere between her esophagus and her trachea. She could see it in Ed's eyes. Something was wrong. And if it was wrong enough for Ed to break their little makeshift code of avoidance, then it had to be very wrong.

"What happened?" she blurted far too strongly.

Ed held out his palms in the universal sign for "stop." "No, it's not—it's nothing too bad. I mean—I don't know. . . . I can't tell, but. . ." Ed's eyes darted over to Chris and then back to Gaia. "Can we. . . talk

169

alone?" He gave a nod to Chris. "Sorry," he said. "It will only take a second."

Chris gave Ed a quick once-over. "No, it's fine." He smiled.

Ed turned back to Gaia, but she was already shooting up from the stoop. Whatever was wrong, she wanted to know about it immediately.

THE SILENCE WAS SICKENING. IT

was quickly becoming so much worse than anything Ed could possibly have to say. Not to mention the proximity problem. Being face-to-face with Ed's eyes reflecting

Anesthetized Smile

the glaring sun was leaving Gaia with a slew of indiscernible feelings that she very much wanted to sweep away. His hands were thrust deep in the low-hanging pockets of his jeans, and his hair was doing the messy thing it always did, and everything about him was so completely Ed that it was reminding Gaia of everything. Which was exactly why avoidance and distance were really the only way to go.

"I, uh. . . ," Ed stammered.

170

"Look, just say it," Gaia said, far more harshly than she had intended. Ed's eyes widened with surprise. A wave of guilt shot down her back. "I'm—I'm sorry; that wasn't supposed to—"

"No, it's okay," Ed assured her. "You always snap when you're feeling. . ." Ed shut himself up and glanced in five different directions before facing her eyes again. He knew everything about her. Everything. God, this was depressing.

"Are you sure you're okay?" he asked.

Gaia crossed her arms tightly to her chest, as if that would somehow keep the thousand thoughts running through her head from slipping out. "I'm fine," she said, tight-lipped. "Look, Ed, if it's not serious, then let's just—"

"It's Heather," Ed said.

Gaia blinked hard and tried to force herself to breathe easily. "What happened to Heather?" she asked.

"She's fine. She was just. . . She was worried about you and. . . she asked me to give you a message, and so. . . I said I would. I mean, I know we're not supposed to be—"

"Well, what happened?" Gaia interrupted. Her focus switched instantly to Heather, which at least helped her shove all those indiscernible Ed feelings back where they belonged. If anything else tragic had happened to Heather because of Gaia, she wasn't sure

171

if she'd be able to deal. "Did something happen to her?" Gaia's foot began to tap repeatedly against the sidewalk. Ed had to give her a piece of actual information that would break this unbearable tension.

"I'm not totally sure," he said.

"Well, did something *happen* or *didn't* it?"

"Jesus, I'm *trying* to tell you—will you just give me a *chance*?"

Dead silence. Gaia felt another bolt of guilt shoot down her spine. She took a deep breath and tried to relax. But it wasn't working. "I'm sorry, Ed, I'm not trying to—"

"I know." Ed took a long, deep breath of his own. "I do know. I'm just trying to give you a message, Gaia, that's it, okay? Heather couldn't reach you at home, and the only person she could think of to call was me. I don't think she understood that we don't. . ." He blew out a puff of air and shoved his hands deeper in his pockets. "Here's the message. She said that some people came to visit her up at the school. Two men, I think. And she said they were asking a lot of questions. Questions about you, about your uncle. She said they were harassing her. She said she was worried that they might be coming to talk to you, and she thought that could be dangerous for you, maybe. . . . I guess that's it. I don't think they wanted her to tell you about them. I think they told her not to tell you about them. Do you think it's really bad, or—?"

"Was that all she said?"

"Well. . . I think she was pretty scared. But. . . a couple of guys asking some questions? That's not necessarily the end of the world, is it? I mean, I don't know. You know how your life works, and. . . I guess I could never really figure it out. Is this really bad or what?"

Gaia was silent.

"Gaia. . . ? Are you okay?"

That was a fair question. Because in spite of herself, Gaia had basically ceased to move. She was for all intents and purposes frozen solid. Her brain had done the math in about two seconds. Oliver's warning at the boardinghouse that night. . . about two men asking questions—two men he didn't trust, two men who had made him deeply suspicious, maybe even a little frightened. She'd been convinced that he was being paranoid—on edge after everything he'd been through with the Agency. She'd been absolutely sure that they were just CIA asking a few perfunctory follow-up questions.

But now she wasn't so sure. Now she wasn't sure at all. Now she was only sure of one thing. This little message from Heather had left her with one very sickening, depressing, pathetic, and most inevitable thought:

It was starting again.

Something. Something was beginning. Someone was starting another round of nightmares for Gaia

173

Moore. Not just Gaia, but everyone around her. As per usual. She was sure of it. She could just feel it. She could practically feel the hook digging into her back. She could feel herself being cast out into the water, and she could feel them coming. Sharks, piranhas, anything with teeth. Anything that could smell her out, track her down, rip her into pieces, and swallow her up.

Two men looking like CIA and asking a bunch of intimidating questions—that had to be the Organization. That was their MO. Everything about it reeked of the Organization. Was Yuri still giving orders from prison? Or Natasha? Tatiana? Somehow, some way? Obviously Oliver was out of the running. Loki totally would have started an operation this way, but there *was* no more Loki. But what about the others? Did they still even have them all in custody?

Which one of them was it this time? And what did they want? And *why*? These were the questions that Gaia would clearly be asking for as long as she lived—as long as she walked the earth.

Gaia Moore. . . this is your life. You know it. You've always known it.

Thoughts of new Gaia were burning up into cinders like useless wads of newspaper in a fire.

"Gaia? Jesus, are you home?" Ed was peering deeper into her eyes. "Is it really that bad? Come on. Tell me it's not that bad."

"No, Ed," she said finally. "No, it's not that bad. Don't

even worry about it. I'll give Heather a call. Thanks." She was numb now. Maybe she could just stay numb for the rest of her days. Fearless and numb. *Ms. Anesthetic 2003. Step right up and check out the human vegetable. She won't react to positive or negative stimuli. She won't react to anything. Go ahead. Throw a brick at her head and see what happens. . . .*

She had nothing more to say to Ed. That was the absolute here. Ed would never again be dragged into this five-year-long tragedy. Never. As far as Ed needed to know, everything was just absolutely, unequivocally *fine*.

Ed, you go find Kai, and you two have a nice life. Maybe I'll see you someday in heaven or wherever.

"I gotta go," Gaia uttered. "Thanks for passing on the info." She pasted a lame Stepford-like smile on her face.

Ed stared at her for about five long seconds. "Sure," he said tentatively.

And in the moment that followed, their eyes proceeded to have a lengthy and complex conversation about the entire history of their relationship and how and why they had gotten to this most depressing point. And the end of that unspoken conversation was clear: Ed knew Gaia far too well to buy her anesthetized smile. He knew there was much more going on in her head than she was letting on. But he understood: it had nothing to do with him anymore. It couldn't. It couldn't for both of their sakes, and somehow they had each come to accept it. So, with her smile, Gaia silently begged Ed to leave it alone. And Ed silently agreed to pretend to believe her.

"So... bye, I guess," Ed said.

"Bye," she muttered.

And Ed turned around, and Gaia turned around. And that was that. Reluctant and awkward discussion from hell over.

Ed made a beeline for the school doors, and Gaia walked back toward Chris, who was still waiting for her on the stoop across the street. She could barely feel her feet or her hands as she walked. Or anything else, for that matter.

"What was that all about?" Chris was examining Gaia's demeanor carefully.

"Oh, nothing," Gaia said, standing stock still like a robot. "That was totally nothing."

"Wait a minute. . . ." Chris got up off the stoop and took a step closer. He leaned his perfect face closer to Gaia's, and then he raised his delicate index finger up to her cheek. "Is that a tear?" He wiped the tear from her face as his expression grew more and more concerned.

"What? No," Gaia insisted. She swiped at her cheeks quickly. She hadn't been the least bit aware that tears had begun to stream slowly from her eyes. It was the numb person's version of crying. Tears without a hint of emotion. Her body knew she was losing it even when she did not. And now she was embarrassed to all hell. She didn't want to show anything. Not a thing.

"Gaia, come on, *talk to me*," Chris insisted. Now he had dispensed completely with his usual bright-eyed humor. Now he was 100 percent serious. "What is going on with you? You *have* to let me help you."

"*Why?*" Gaia heard herself cry. It had come entirely from out of nowhere, this sudden regurgitation of raw emotion. It must have been building up this entire time, just waiting to burst through her stone face the first chance it got. And now it was pouring out. To *Chris Rodke* of all people. A boy she hardly knew. It was downright mortifying. But Gaia couldn't seem to locate the turnoff mechanism at this point. Now the whole thing was unreeling, whether she wanted it to or not. "Why do you want to hear any of this?" she moaned. "You don't need this kind of crap in your perfect life, Chris. You just don't. I'm not worth the effort, believe me. *Run,* Chris. Tell your sister. Run while you can, before you end up like that poor son of a bitch who just walked back through those doors."

"Okay, *stop*," Chris bellowed. "Just stop. Stop and stay quiet and listen."

Something about Chris's kind and commanding tone did the trick. Gaia quieted herself down and locked onto Chris's self-assured eyes.

"I don't know *what* you were just talking about," he said calmly. "I have no idea what you did or didn't do to Ed over there, and I have no idea who or *what* has turned you into this sad tortured soul. But you know what? I don't *need* to know. The details don't matter. The point is, I've been there, Gaia. I used to *hate* who I was. I hated myself. I was ashamed of my money, I was ashamed of being gay, and I just felt generally screwed by life. So you know what I did? I *changed* it. Me. *I* changed my life. I got some therapy, I started enjoying my money and spending it everywhere and on everyone I could, and I came the hell out of the closet.

"Gaia, what did I tell you in that hotel? What did I say? You said people never change—well, I say that is complete and utter bullshit. The only reason people don't change is that deep down inside, they don't really want to. But you're not them, Gaia, I can see that. You're dying to change. You're dying to transform. If you don't like your life, then change it. *You* have the power. Stop telling me all this crap about being cursed. Stop handing all the responsibility over to fate. Your life doesn't control you—*you* control *it*. If there's something about you that's holding you back from the life that you want, then don't just sit around lamenting it. Don't just sit there in the closet like I did and wallow in it. You go right now and you *fix* it. Right now. Because you can. Because you're in control."

Gaia went totally silent. Chris Rodke certainly did like his speeches. But she had nothing against speeches when they were so completely, indisputably right. And that was the point of Gaia's silence. Not resistance, not doubt or disbelief. Just sheer unadulterated agreement.

Her whole damn life was always about *them*. It was always about what *they* were going to do to her next or to the people she loved. It was always about what thousand-ton weight the Fates were going to drop on her next. Everything always *happened* to Gaia. And Gaia never made anything happen.

But Dr. Ulrich was just sitting there, holding the key. The key to taking control of her own life. The key to giving those asshole Fates the finger once and for all. Along with all the rest of the scumbags and schemers out there just waiting to sink their teeth in. The nightmare cycle of Gaia's life didn't have to start again. It didn't. No one had to ask any more questions about her if there was nothing to ask about. And no one had to get hurt anymore if there was no reason to hurt them. Nothing had to start again.

Not if she stopped it.

"Thank you, Chris," Gaia said as she began moving down the street.

"Wait, where are you going?" he laughed.

"I'm going to fix it," she called back to him. "I'm going to fix it all right now."

He hadn't
counted on
the glimpse
of her
tangled hair
out of the
corner of
his eye.

love
and
hate

GAIA RAN DOWN THE EMPTY SIDEWALK

A Decision

on East Twenty-first Street. It was early evening, and the dusk light was fading. The small brownstone apartment buildings all had smooth stone faces, and their windows reflected the pale sky. It was a beautiful neighborhood, there was no two ways about it—and extremely expensive. When Robert Rodke had said that he'd "dragged" Dr. Ulrich away from Princeton University, he must have used a checkbook to do the dragging.

Gaia had made up her mind.

It was as simple as that: she'd come to a decision. All by herself, thinking it through, she'd reasoned what she had to do. Sure, Ed's message—the crazy warning from Heather Gannis, of all people—had made a difference. So had Chris Rodke's strong words. But in the end, this was *her* decision.

She had had enough. *No more,* she thought firmly. No more danger for herself and her friends and family. No more threat of being different from everyone else. It had been way too long.

I'm sorry, Heather. I'm sorry they scared you, whoever they were. But it's ending now.

Gaia was looking at the addresses, trying to find Dr. Ulrich's house. There were loud party sounds coming from one of the brownstones across the street—a fairly rambunctious cocktail party, it

181

sounded like. Getting closer, Gaia realized that the sounds were coming from the Ulrich residence.

Here goes, Gaia thought, crossing the street toward the house. There was no traffic. The quiet street was entirely still, except for the party sounds.

Gaia wondered if she would always remember this day the rest of her life. She realized that she probably would. Looking back over all of it she was amazed: all the love and hate and fighting and running and struggling, the life of a girl who had done nothing to deserve any of it, who had just been born without the fear gene.

Am I doing the right thing, Mom? Gaia thought, climbing the brownstone steps. She had no way of knowing what her mother would have said had she been there. But she thought that she knew. Gaia's mother would have wanted her to be happy. That was all.

Gaia's mother would have understood.

The street was so peaceful and still, it was like an oil painting. Gaia could see lots of men and women inside the brownstone's living room, inside the curtained windows.

And what would her father say? Gaia realized she didn't know. *Guess what, Dad? I'm finally free.* Would he hug her and say that he loved her and that she'd done the right thing? Gaia was sure of it. She knew that she was guessing, but still, she was sure.

Finally free.

Gaia rang the doorbell.

It took a moment, and then the big, glossy door swung open. The party sounds got much louder. A handsome middle-aged woman in a green dress stood there, holding a glass of white wine. Behind her, Gaia could see dozens of men and women, the men in suits, the women in dresses. All were talking and laughing; piano music was coming from somewhere.

The woman looked at Gaia dubiously. "Yes?" she said.

"I'm here to see Dr. Ulrich," Gaia said steadily. "I need to talk to him."

"I'm sorry," the woman said. She wore diamond earrings, Gaia saw. She had a thick German accent. "The doctor is busy right now. We are hosting friends, as you see."

"Please tell him it's Gaia Moore," Gaia said, "and it's important. He'll understand."

The woman frowned at Gaia and then held up a finger and gently eased the door closed. Gaia stood and waited. In the distance a car horn honked. She could hear the voices of the partygoers, discussing whatever middle-aged adults discussed at parties.

The door opened again. Dr. Ulrich stood there. He wore an expensive-looking double-breasted suit and a red silk tie. His hair was neatly combed. The suit made him look even shorter somehow.

"Ms. Moore," Dr. Ulrich said. "What a pleasant surprise. We are entertaining, as you can see; it is not the most convenient—"

"It's *my* blood," Gaia said.

Dr. Ulrich stared back at her.

"The blood I gave you," she went on. "The strange chromosome. It's me."

She expected him to look surprised, but oddly, he didn't. "Yes," he said evenly.

"I was born without it," Gaia went on. "That gene. And it's ruined my whole life."

"Yes. . . yes," Ulrich said. Again he seemed lost in thought, as he had at his laboratory before.

"You knew it was me?" Gaia was surprised.

"Of course!" Ulrich frowned severely. "Do you think me a fool? Blond hair, blue eyes, right-handed. . . I was looking directly at your *chromosomes,* young lady. You cannot hide under such circumstances. It was clearly your blood."

"Oh." Gaia hadn't thought of that. "Listen, I won't keep you. But there's a reason I'm here. I want—I want you to fix it. I want you to do what you said before: I want you to make me normal. To make me whole."

Ulrich stood there, just outside his glossy front door, staring at her. The party sounds continued inside. The sky was dimmer now; evening was advancing.

"You understand," Ulrich said, "that such a procedure cannot be reversed."

"Yes."

"This is not a trivial matter, Ms. Moore. And further,

think of the benefits of your unusual condition," Ulrich went on. "There is no shame in being different. The spectrum of human variation is a splendid benefit to us all. Every person, regardless of their strengths and weaknesses, is part of the tapestry of the human species. And it is a remarkable thing. . . to have no fear. It makes you a most special person. Think of what you can achieve if you—"

"No," Gaia said. "No. You don't know what it's like. You don't have any way of knowing. I've been living with this all my life. I'm done with it."

And hearing herself say it, Gaia realized that she'd never been as sure of anything in her life. *I'm done with it—for good.*

Ulrich sighed heavily. He took off his glasses and started cleaning them. When he turned his brown eyes on Gaia, they seemed startlingly `piercing and direct.`

"I must ask that you do something," Ulrich said. "For my own conscience. I'm afraid this is not negotiable; it is a condition that you must agree to."

"All right," Gaia said dubiously. She had no idea what Ulrich was going to ask for. Money? The chance to publish his results? The opportunity to have colleagues in the scientific community observe his work as he showed off the famous "fearless" girl?

But what Ulrich said next took Gaia completely by surprise.

"Ms. Moore, I must ask that you find somebody whom you trust," Ulrich said. "Someone close to you. A parent or a friend or a loved one of some kind. And when you find that person, go to him or her and ask what they think. Ask for their counsel, their advice. Ask this person to please think about what you are about to do and tell you if it is advisable."

"But I can't do that," Gaia argued. "I can't reveal what—"

"Then I will not proceed." Ulrich put his glasses back on. "That is that. I will not perform such a drastic, irreversible procedure on the basis of a teenager's whim, no matter how passionately you want it. I must insist that you get advice."

"But—"

"Find someone you trust, Gaia," Ulrich urged. He had stepped closer; Gaia could barely see the details of his silk tie in the fading light. The tie was decorated with tiny DNA strands, she saw. Very clever. "Find this person and get his or her advice. Once you have done this and you are *sure,* then come find me at the hospital, where we are completing our genetic lab facility."

"Okay."

"And I will give you fear," Ulrich concluded. "Fair enough?"

"Fair enough," Gaia said softly. "Thank you."

"I must rejoin my guests," Ulrich said, his hand on

the doorknob. "I would invite you in, but you are not of the drinking age, are you?"

"That's right," Gaia said. It was nearly dark now—the city's evening wind was picking up. "I'm sorry to bother you at home, Dr. Ulrich. Thanks for everything."

"Just do what I have asked," Ulrich said. He pulled open his door—the bright light and party sounds flooded out. "And perhaps we shall see each other again soon."

Gaia had nothing to say. She stood there on the brownstone steps as the door closed, and then she turned away, gazing at the street, and began to move down the wide steps and away toward the boardinghouse—toward home.

I've had a kind of a revelation.

Maybe that's too strong a word. Call it just a "realization." Anyway, I've figured something out.

My great curse—and I'll carry it with me the rest of my life—is that I remember everything I've done. For years I was somebody else: a loathsome, despicable man named Loki, who ruthlessly masterminded a criminal organization. In that role, which was forged out of my immature bitterness and fury when I was young, I shamelessly manipulated and exploited all the people around me. Some of those people were pawns—henchmen, spies, assassins, scientists—and some of them were my loved ones. My family, my closest kin. My brother. My brother's wife. My niece.

It wasn't hard. I turned my intelligence to the task, and I figured out a foolproof system. I called it "the first principle,"

because that's how it was taught
to me. In my supreme arrogance I
congratulated myself for my bril-
liance. I turned everyone so that
they worked for me, even though
they thought they were working
for themselves.

It was wrong. It was evil.

But I'm still doing it.

Look at me now. I'm trying to
save Gaia because she's in danger. Am I capable of saving her?
I think so. Am I willing, determined to protect her? More than
anything. She's my brother's
daughter. I owe her my life. Yes,
I owe her everything. She's my
one chance to make up for all the
harm I've done.

So I *must* save her. I *can* save her.

Whoever those two vermin are—
Rowan and Morrow—and whoever
they're working for, they won't
get near her.

But what have I done so far?

Nothing. Nothing that's effec-
tive. All I've done is convince
her that I'm unhinged. I've wan-
dered around Manhattan like a

middle-aged fool, showing up at her boardinghouse and trying to convince her to believe me.

It's just "the first principle" again. Get her on my side. Persuade her that I'm right. It's Loki all over again.

I'm being stupid.

I'm acting like some kind of self-obsessed would-be mentor, thinking that I have to *convince* her of something, when what I should be doing is using my real resources. I spent *years* building my network of operatives. Skilled men and women in complex, secret "sleeper" networks, who will do what I need them to do.

Since I got rid of Loki—and abandoned everything that name meant—I've avoided using them whenever possible. I thought that reactivating my networks would be the same as becoming Loki again.

But that's stupid, like I said. Loki wasn't Loki because of a few henchmen. He was who he was because of his arrogance—his belief that he could change people's minds. But I

never really changed Gaia's mind
about anything. No, I can't change
Gaia's mind.

But I can protect her.

That's what I'll do. What am I
afraid of? My team is still
there. These people are willing
to wait for years between march-
ing orders. Our communications
systems are foolproof. All I have
to do is pick up the phone and
say some code words, and I'm back
in business.

It doesn't mean I'm Loki. It
just means I'm using the resources
at my disposal. And it's for such
a good cause—the urgent need to
protect my wonderful, beautiful,
irreplaceable niece.

Sure.

Did I call it a curse—the fact
that I remember everything I've
done? That's wrong. Yes, I still
wake up screaming in the night,
burdened by nightmares of the
crimes I've committed. I remember
all of that clearly.

But that's not all I remember.
I remember my operatives' pass-

words and activation codes.

And I'm going to use them. I'm going to put my pieces on the board. I'm going to use my men to protect Gaia. They'll follow her, spy on her, and report where she goes. And if she gets into trouble, I'll be ready to save her. It doesn't matter whether she trusts me or not. That's just arrogance. What's important is results.

Like I said, I've had a realization.

I'll pick up the phone, and in just a few hours Gaia will have a dozen secret angels protecting her.

I should have done this long ago.

SOMETIMES THE PARK WAS THE ONLY

A Chorus of Sopranos

place Ed could go to clear his mind and think. It calmed him somehow, particularly when everything was in full swing, which today it was. A crowd had gathered by the shut-down fountain to watch Magic Bob do his act. The chess tables were packed. The hippies had gathered in a circle up on the grass to listen to one of their tie-dyed brothers play a medley of Phish and Grateful Dead tunes. The benches were lined with NYU intellectuals, flipping through the dog-eared used books they'd just bought at the Strand. And most importantly, there were the skaters.

Ed had pretty much sworn off skating after his accident, but that didn't make it any less beautiful to watch. Sometimes, when one of the kids pulled off a perfect maneuver, Ed could actually feel it. It was the ultimate sense memory: his feet pressed against the board, the sound of the wind flying by his ears as he prepped for the landing. . . .

But memories were playing way too large a role in Ed's life these days. He was getting stuck on memories. All kinds of them. Memories of good old Shred on his board, who couldn't have cared less about anything but a good jump and enough money for fries at the McDonald's on

Broadway, memories of his freshman year with Heather, when it had all been about the scruffiest skate rat at school going out with the most stunningly gorgeous princess. And then, of course, there was that other girl. The angriest, darkest, most screwed-up girl that he had ever had the pleasure of eating doughnuts with.

But that really felt like another life now. All of it did. It felt far away. It felt gone. And that feeling—the feeling of loss—was starting to kill Ed's usual life buzz far too often these days. So he was counting on the park to bring the buzz back. He was counting on the shafts of late day sun that cut through the trees. He was counting on the slight smell of green coming from the long branches hanging over his bench on the west side of the path.

But he hadn't counted on the glimpse of her tangled hair out of the corner of his eye. No, he hadn't counted on that. He hadn't counted on seeing her forceful strides as she walked into the MacDougal entrance of the park and moved closer and closer to his bench. What could be a quicker way to send him falling back into a world of buzz-killing memories than to see Gaia Moore herself?

After yesterday's little fiasco of a conversation, Ed had honestly hoped not to run into Gaia again for a while. A long while. He far preferred to hang on to the pleasant memories of their past and flush their new crappy-ass dynamic right down the toilet. He'd learned his lesson while trying to pass on Heather's message yesterday. He had learned that distance and avoidance with Gaia were *unquestionably* the right way to go. The simplest bit of contact just brought back memories of their entire past, and it made their present feel like a goddamn trip to the dentist for a root canal minus the novocaine. Gaia's troubles were her own. They were none of Ed's business now. And his troubles were *his* own. None of *her* business. And that was going to be the basic scheme of things from here on in.

Ed really wished that Gaia would just walk right by him right now. He wished she would walk straight through to the center of the park and right through the arch and out of sight. He was sure that was what she was going to do. But as usual with Gaia Moore, Ed had it all wrong. Instead, she marched straight up to his bench. And she sat down right next to him.

This was not distance. This was not avoidance. This was just deeply and painfully uncomfortable. Ed could not even locate the words for a civil salutation. But Gaia Moore surprised him yet again. She surprised him with an `inexplicably kind tone` and an ease that she had not displayed around him in weeks and weeks. It was downright bizarre.

"I know," she said. It was a strange first thing to say, but somehow, in Gaia's case, it fit. She stared out at West Fourth Street as they sat side by side in the sun. "I know it's all completely screwed up, Ed. Why am I sitting here right now? What am I doing here after that ridiculously crappy encounter yesterday? I know."

"I didn't say anything," Ed replied. He focused on a group of little kids across the path, giggling at the tops of their lungs as they chased each other in tiny circles with bright orange water guns. He had to focus on something other than her face. Because, goddamn her, she still looked so freaking exquisite. He'd glimpsed it once already and that had been enough. The tiny beige freckles on the edges of her nose, the ten different shades of blond dancing over her face in the breeze, the crayon blue color of her eyes when she sat in the sun. . . it was all such a miserable pain in his ass.

"It's a mess, Ed," she said. "Our whole thing—the whole thing; it's just a hideous, unwatchable car wreck."

"Hey, don't candy-coat it for me," Ed said.

"You're right," she muttered. "That doesn't do it justice, does it?"

The kids upped the stakes by leaping on top of and under the benches, ducking for cover and jumping down into huge clumsy tumbles in the dirt. Ed was jealous. Jealous and painfully curious to know why Gaia had sat down next to him on this bench and begun something very closely resembling a conversation.

Cut to the chase, Fargo. Cut to the chase and move on. . . .

"Is this about Heather?" he asked. There was next to no inflection in his voice.

"No." She sighed. "No, this—it's about me, Ed." With that, she made an abrupt move to face him on the bench, shoving her knee up on the seat and hanging her arm over the back. Ed suddenly felt that he had no choice but to face her, too. To stay facing outward would have felt too childish, like some kind of sulking little kid instead of the man he was—a man who was *perfectly* capable of having a polite and functional conversation with his ex-everything.

Yeah. You keep telling yourself that. Maybe you can at least get her *to buy it.*

But the moment he turned to face her, he realized that something really was different this time. Something in her eyes, and therefore something in his, too. Their eyes locked and things just changed. Like that.

Not that the violins swelled. Not that a chorus of sopranos started warbling in the background or anyone began moving in slow motion. It wasn't that. It wasn't romantic. It was just. . . okay. For the first time in so long, Gaia and Ed were face-to-face and it was somehow okay. Why? Ed had no idea. There was no clear-cut reason really, no rational explanation. Ed only knew that he had no desire to screw it up or sabotage it, because it had sent an overwhelming sense of relief flooding through his chest. Like he had been immersed underwater for weeks and had finally gotten his first taste of oxygen. There were no smiles exchanged, no unnecessary apologies. But there was air and there was quiet. Like someone had just smacked the radio and gotten rid of the excruciating static that had been poisoning every one of their previous exchanges.

"I'm not really—" Gaia cut herself off. She seemed displeased with her start, and so she began again. "Ed, I want to ask you something. And. . . it won't really make any sense. And I won't really be able to make it any clearer if you ask me to. But I still want to ask it."

Ed raised a brow in confusion. "What's going on?"

"Don't worry, it's not—look, just skip over the weirdness, okay? The only way this conversation is going to work is if you just skip over the weirdness and listen."

Ed had no response to that, clever or otherwise. He was sure he could find it in his heart to skip over the weirdness, except for the fact that each word out of her mouth only seemed to get weirder.

"Why don't you just tell me what's on your mind," he suggested. "Because you're kind of freaking me out right now."

"I'm trying to tell you," she said. "Just. . . just bear with me." She took a deep breath. "Okay. Ed, if. . . if I wanted to do something drastic. Something drastic that could really change my life—that could really make me. . . you know. . . happy. But it would mean that I'd be. . . different. I mean, different forever. Then do you think I'd be making the right choice?"

Ed cocked his head. "Gaia. . . are you speaking in code or something?"

"*No*," she snapped. "Jesus, Ed. No, I'm not speaking in code. I just can't be *specific*, that's all. Is that a *problem* for you?"

"Hey, wait a minute," Ed shot back. "Now you're yelling at me? What the hell is the matter with you? First you walk up out of nowhere, drop down next to me on this bench like we're suddenly good buddies again or something, and then you throw all these weird Martian disclaimers at me, and then you start speaking in code. And now you're *pissed* at me?"

"I *told* you that it wouldn't make sense, Ed. That was the first thing I said."

"Since when are we even speaking, Gaia?"

"Since yesterday."

"Yesterday? You call that speaking? That was not speaking; that was something else. That was, like, a failed UN peace conference or something. Everybody speaking different languages and no one even wanting to speak in the first place."

"Fine, then we're speaking now, okay? Now we're speaking."

"*Why?* Why now? Why are you speaking to me right now? Why are you here?"

"Because I *trust* you, Ed! Because you are the only person I. . . Because you are the only person. . . who

199

knows me. . . really." Gaia dropped both her legs back down on the ground and turned away from Ed.

If she'd been looking for a way to shut him up, then she'd found it. Ed could only sit there and stare at her cinematic profile, watching her take a series of short frustrated breaths. How exactly could he speak now? What exactly was he supposed to say to that? It was the nicest thing she'd said to him in weeks. Maybe months. Maybe it was the nicest thing she had ever said to him.

"I'm sorry," he said, though he had no idea what he was sorry for. No, that wasn't true. Maybe he'd gotten a little hostile there for a second. But so had she. This whole thing was far too weird to analyze anyway.

But Ed was beginning to understand how important this conversation was to Gaia. Even if he had absolutely no understanding of what it was about. And whatever the hell they were—friends, enemies, exes, distant acquaintances—she was still Gaia, and he was still Ed. And maybe that was her point. Maybe that was why she had come to him in the first place to ask this superhypothetical completely unintelligible question that sounded to him like absolute gibberish. And so maybe he just needed to try and answer it. And leave it at that.

"Okay," Ed said. "Okay, ask me again."

She huffed out a few more frustrated breaths and then she finally turned back to him. Ed was starting to see just how difficult it must have been for her to come to him like this, particularly given the disastrous state of their relationship up until this point. It suddenly made him far more determined to be kind.

"Okay," Gaia said. She looked into Ed's eyes. "I want to do something. I want to do something that's going to change my life."

"And you can't tell me what it is."

"I can't tell you what it is."

Ed let out a long sigh and tried to accept this fact. "Okay. . ."

"And if I do it. . . it means that I'm going to change, Ed. Permanently."

"Change how?"

Gaia scanned the park, as if she were taking it in for the last time or something. It made Ed deeply uncomfortable. "I don't know for sure," she said. "I'm just going to change. Maybe I'll be a little less. . . brave."

"Well, you've got plenty of that to spare."

"I don't know, Ed. I don't know. I might be a little less. . . me. But my life would be. . . clearer. I mean, easier. Not jam-packed with one stupid tragedy after the other."

Ed suddenly felt slightly ill. This was, after all, the only thing he had ever wanted. For Gaia, for him, for *them*. If he had ever once believed that she was capable of making those changes in her life, then he never would have—

But he wasn't going to say that. Now was not the time to say that. Maybe there would never be a time to say that. He took a good long look at Gaia and made sure she was clear on this one. "Gaia, if you mean what you say—if you really believe that this *thing* you're going to do could have that effect on your life—then you need to do it. I don't know if you're looking for my 'blessing' or what. But if that is what you're looking for. . . then you have it."

Gaia didn't exactly smile. But her face registered a certain kind of relief and gratitude. "I guess maybe that *was* what I was looking for," she said. "Thank you, Ed. For. . . well, just thanks." She held her gaze on Ed. And then she finally glanced down at her watch. "I should go." She stood up off the bench.

"Can I just ask you one question?" Ed knew it wasn't a particularly appropriate question to ask, but at this point he couldn't help himself.

"Okay," she agreed reluctantly.

"Well. . . shouldn't Jake be the one you talk to about this 'whatever it is'? Why didn't you ask Jake?"

Gaia looked slightly uncomfortable. "Jake's a huge part of why I want to do this," she said.

For some reason that hurt. It probably hurt more than it should have. "Right." Ed nodded. "Of course he is."

"And you," she added. "And Sam. Because none of you deserves what I've put you through, Ed. No one does."

Ed couldn't argue with that. He just wished she had figured it out a little sooner.

Gaia backed away slowly, keeping her eyes on Ed as she headed for the exit.

"Gaia," he called to her. "Are you sure? About this 'thing'? Have you looked at it from every possible angle? Are you sure it's the right thing to do?"

"I'm sure," she called back. "Really, Ed." With that she turned around and walked until she'd disappeared behind the bushes at the edge of the park.

Ed felt exhilarated and uneasy and strange. It was the longest, most important conversation he'd ever had without having any idea what he was talking about. But then again, that pretty much defined his entire friendship with Gaia Moore. Long, important, and impossible to understand.

From: gaia13@alloymail.com
To: jakem@alloymail.com
Time: 4:48 P.M.
Re: I suck

Jake,

I know. I suck. I'm not avoiding you, I swear.
But it probably looks like I am and that's my fault.

Everything is just insane right now, Jake.
Everything is crazy.

But I do have some good news. It turns out my dad
is going to have a little time off to see me. Just
an overnight thing, but still, I think it could
really do some serious wonders for me to go see him.

So the thing is, that means I'm going to be gone
overnight and through tomorrow. But when I get
back, if this little trip goes the way I hope it
goes, then I think I will definitely be a lot more
clearheaded than I have been the last few days.

What I mean is, I really want to finish our
conversation, Jake. I really do. And if this trip
goes the way I think it will go, then the first
thing I want to do when I get back is finish that
conversation. Seriously. FIRST thing.

Just give me twenty-four hours before you
start getting pissed. Twenty-four hours. That's
all I need.

—G.

SURVEILLANCE FIELD REPORT

To: Central Control [Oliver Moore]
From: FALCON [Operative #451, Manhattan Unit]
Transmitted via secure SATCOM encrypted lines at 20:04:30 EST

REPORT FOLLOWS

Sir,

As ordered, subject acquired at 13:06:20 in and around premises of the Village School in lower Manhattan. With the assistance of support agents RAVEN and SPARROW, operative secured full surveillance of the location to ensure that target did not leave the school property unnoticed.

At 15:30:01 subject departed the Village School and traveled on foot to Washington Square Park. Subject remained there for approximately twenty minutes while under full surveillance, clearly unaware of being watched as she conversed with an unidentified male schoolmate. The acquisition of sound recordings of this conversation was not possible given the extremely short lead time of the mission, but if so ordered, this operative (and support agents RAVEN and SPARROW) can easily begin full audio monitoring of target.

After completing the conversation with the unidentified schoolmate, subject departed on foot from Washington Square Park, traveling west across Manhattan.

At the present moment, as this secure report is being transmitted, subject is still traveling on foot, making her way toward the hospital buildings near Twelfth Street. Support Agent RAVEN attests that subject's facial expression betrayed hints of determination and conviction, but this is pure speculation. Although subject destination and purpose cannot be conclusively determined, it is this agent's opinion that subject is on her way to the hospital.

Operatives RAVEN and SPARROW will continue to maintain surveillance, and this unit will report any changes as soon as they occur.

FALCON

Addendum: On behalf of the team, it's a pleasure to be working for you again, sir.

END REPORT

AND HERE SHE WAS, ON HER WAY.

Wouldn't Have Time to Scream

Walking toward the hospital where they would give her fear.

Gaia felt very strange. Some of it was the conversation with Ed. It gave her a feeling of peace to have talked to him the way she just had— to hear his voice, see his kind eyes, and realize again how much he meant to her.

The sky was dark. The stars, as always, were invisible. In New York you never saw the stars; it was a fact of life.

The streets were full of traffic as always. Gaia thought about the city and about the role it had played in her life. If Tom Moore had lived somewhere else, if Katia had come over from Russia and not chosen to become a singer here, in Manhattan, would they have met? If they hadn't met, they wouldn't have a daughter. Would her life have been the same vivid, savage cocktail of love and betrayal and violence and beauty and death? Gaia didn't know, would never know.

Crossing Greenwich Village, Gaia found herself thinking back over her life. It was strange, this mood she'd been in since she'd met Dr. Ulrich—since this whole thing began. It was strange how her desire to be new Gaia had come true, and so much faster than she'd expected. Mere days after kissing Jake across the lunch-room table, here she was, on her way to keep an appointment to do the impossible—to change herself forever.

To become whole.

Gaia could see the flanks of St. Vincent's hospital ahead of her. She realized she was walking more quickly, as if she couldn't wait to get inside and do this thing—as if she was afraid somebody would stop her. Which was crazy, because there wasn't anyone trying to stop her. Ed Fargo had given her his blessing. Jake had gotten her e-mail, and while she felt bad about misleading him (okay, lying to him), it just wasn't something he could understand. He hadn't known her long enough to understand. And her father was unavailable. After all the times that people had interfered with her life and tried to make her do things she didn't want to do, she was finally doing something purely for herself. . . and there really *wasn't* anyone who could stop her.

Gaia moved down the sidewalk in front of St. Vincent's, where Dr. Ulrich's team from Rodke and Simon had set up their genetics facilities. She could feel her heart rate speeding up as she approached the glass doors. She was almost there. Soon she would—

"Gaia!"

A familiar voice. Right behind her.

Oliver.

Gaia's heart sank. This was absolutely, positively the last thing she needed.

Gaia turned around.

She was shocked by Oliver's appearance. Her uncle looked *awful*. She had noticed before how the lines on his face had become more pronounced. Now he looked absolutely craggy. His hair was wild, and his eyes looked bloodshot and reddened. His clothes were disheveled, and he was out of breath. He stood there on the sidewalk, the headlights of passing cars shining on his beige windbreaker as he pleadingly looked at her.

"Gaia, thank God I got here in time."

What the hell?

"In time for what?" Gaia asked.

"To stop you," Oliver rasped. He was winded, Gaia realized—he must have run over here to catch her. "To stop you from—from going in there."

"Oliver—" Gaia tried to keep a civil tone. But this was beyond irritating. And furthermore, it was *strange*. It was mysterious. And she just didn't want to deal with it. "Oliver, how did you find me? How did you know I was here?"

"Don't worry about that," Oliver barked impatiently. "That's not your concern. I'm here for a reason, like I said. I'm here to stop you."

"But—" Gaia walked closer to her uncle, brushing her wind-tossed hair back from her face. She had to be diplomatic; it was obvious. "But Oliver, why? Why do

209

you want to stop me? What do you know about this? What do you think I'm doing?"

"*I don't know*," Oliver raged. Gaia found herself taking an inadvertent step backward. His face. . . it reminded her of dark memories.

Of Loki.

"I don't know what you're doing here, Gaia. But it's all wrong. Can't you see that? There's something going on here that neither of us understands."

"That's ridiculous," Gaia said firmly. It was funny how fast the words came into her head and how smoothly they came out. Once you'd told one big lie, the next one was *much* easier. "That's just ridiculous, Oliver. I may need to get my appendix out, that's all. You know I never got my appendix removed, and now there's a possibility that—"

"No! No! No!" Oliver's face was overcome with anguish. He reached toward her but then pulled his arms back. "You've never lied to me before, Gaia. You're not a liar. Why start now? Doesn't the fact that you're lying tell you something? Doesn't it tell you that some— that some part of you knows you're making a mistake?"

"I'm not lying," Gaia said patiently. She was trying to figure out the best way to calm Oliver down and persuade him to leave. This was just *not* what she wanted to be doing right now. "Can't you understand that? Even at my age, an appendix can be a problem, and—"

"Gaia!" Oliver took a deep breath, as if struggling

heroically to control his temper. He succeeded. When he spoke again, his voice was remarkably quiet.

"Gaia," Oliver said, "I'm your uncle and I love you. Tom's away, so I have to look out for you. My team found you here and I had to—"

"Your *'team'*?" Gaia was incredulous.

"Find out what you were doing. Please, can't it wait? Give it a day. Give it a day so I can look into it and maybe call Rodriguez and do an investigation. Then if everything's all right, I'll apologize and leave you alone and you can"—Oliver pointed up at the dark flank of the hospital—"go in there and do whatever you want."

"No." Gaia didn't even hesitate. "No. No more—no more surveillance and investigations and waiting. Not this time. No."

And she turned around and started walking toward the hospital doors.

"*Gaia!*" Oliver called after her. He could hear the anguish in his voice as she pushed her way into the bright, air-conditioned hospital lobby. "*Gaia, wait! I'm begging you!*"

"No," Gaia whispered, more to herself than to him. She wouldn't look behind her—she stepped forward, toward the hospital's admittance desk, where several nurses and a security guard were stationed. "No, Oliver—not this time."

"*Gaia!*"

Oliver grabbed her arm. Gaia flinched, but she wouldn't look at him.

"Gaia, you're making a *mistake*," Oliver said. "I don't understand it, but I know you're making some kind of mistake. I'm *absolutely sure of it*. You've got to listen to me and *stop this!*"

Gaia was done listening.

"Excuse me, sir?" Gaia called out to the security guard. "This man's harassing me."

The guard sprang to his feet, his square badge glinting in the fluorescent light as he started toward them. "Sir, leave the young lady alone," he began.

"Gaia, don't," Oliver said behind her. She still wouldn't look at him. "Please."

"Sir, you'll have to leave," the guard told Oliver. He was brandishing his nightstick, obviously unaware that the man he was speaking to could kill him so fast that he wouldn't even have time to scream.

He's going to attack the guard, Gaia thought sadly. She could clearly see it coming. *He's going to snap and attack the guard and hurt him, and then we'll have a big fight, and the cops will come, and it'll all be over for him. And it's all so unnecessary.*

But none of that happened.

She felt Oliver's hand slip from her shoulder.

"Sir," the guard said again. "Please leave the young lady alone."

"All right," Oliver rasped behind her. She could

hear his footsteps moving away. His voice was the voice of utter defeat, of utter despair. "All right, I'm going. Gaia. . . good-bye. I hope with all my heart I'm wrong. And I wish you the best."

"Good-bye," Gaia whispered. She was staring at the wall in front of her, and suddenly she realized that her vision was blurring—she was seeing double because her eyes were brimming with tears.

Good-bye, she thought. *Good-bye to all of it. Good-bye.*

Oliver's footsteps receded behind her as she made her way to the hospital elevator. And when the elevator arrived on the sixth floor and she followed the signs that read Rodke and Simon Laboratories, she saw Dr. Ulrich standing there waiting for her in his spotless lab coat, as they'd arranged. Gaia wiped the tears from her face and gazed straight ahead.

"Welcome, Gaia," the doctor said warmly. "Are you ready?"

"Yes," Gaia said, in a clear, steady voice. "I'm ready."

I've never been readier for anything.

"Then," the doctor said, gesturing toward a set of dark metal doors, "let us begin."

Her fear was
so intense
that it
nearly made
her faint.

**new
Gaia**

Gaia doesn't want to talk.

It's obvious. Only an idiot could miss it. I could pretend that I haven't noticed—that I haven't gotten the message. But after the Mercer Hotel and the Rodkes' party, I'm sure of it. It's not just the way she changes the subject. It's not just the way she won't look me in the eyes when it comes up. Beyond all of that, it's just a feeling I get.

And honestly, I don't mind. It's actually fine.

She may not believe that I mean that. She might think that I'm secretly getting more and more upset and that I'm going to keep bothering her about this big conversation I want to have.

But I'm not. As crazy as it sounds, I can deal with it. I've already learned something about Gaia: basically, it's worth it. It's worth not knowing. Because the way things are between us right now is turning out to be just fine.

So I can respect her wishes.

If Gaia wants to wait before
we sit down and have that "couple" conversation—that "Jake and
Gaia" conversation—I can live
with it. I've tried to make that
clear to her: I honestly can
live with it just as long as she
wants me to. It's not a strain
at all.

But something's wrong.

I'm not exactly sure *what*,
exactly. But there's definitely a
problem of some kind.

It's probably not a big deal,
but I'll feel better once I've
dealt with it. I can already
tell—it's that kind of situation.
The kind where you can't put
something out of your mind until
you've convinced yourself that
you're being crazy—that there's
no problem at all.

I'm not even sure if it has
anything to do with me. In fact,
I kind of think it doesn't. And
if it's *not* about me, then, actually, it's none of my business.
Gaia can have as much of her own

life, away from me, as she wants.
It's not like she's under any
sort of obligation to include me
in anything. If she wants to stay
completely away from me for two
days without really explaining
why, that's fine. It could be
that it's exactly what she said
in that e-mail: wanting to spend
time with her dad. That seems
completely plausible.

Except I don't buy it.

I really have no idea why, but
I'm convinced that something's
up, that something's happening
right in front of me and I can't
see what it is. And whatever that
thing is, it's putting Gaia in
some kind of danger.

And that just changes the
rules. If she's in danger, I've
got to do something. No matter
how much the rules say differ-
ently—the boy-girl rules.

Why an e-mail, anyway? Why not
a face-to-face statement or even
a phone call?

As if she couldn't face me with
the news? As if it was a lie?

I don't want to believe that—
but I have to face the possibility. And if it *is* a lie, then
she's *really* telling me to back
off. . . and I've just got to do
it.

Unless she needs my help.

And I just have this crazy
feeling that's possible. I can't
get the idea out of my head—I
know something's wrong.

Really wrong.

And before things get worse,
I've got to see her. I've *got* to.
That's all.

JAKE CROSSED BANK STREET, MOVING

Inappropriate Touching

toward the front of the Collingwood Residency Hall. It was exactly as he remembered it from three nights before—from the night he'd helped Gaia pack her boxes and move in.

Somehow that seemed like a different century. Like it was immeasurably long ago and everything had changed.

Jake sprinted up the boardinghouse steps. The street was quiet and cool—it had been dark for a while, and the night air beneath the dark trees had finally lost its daytime heat. The orange streetlight shone down like before, illuminating Collingwood's wide, clean steps.

Jake rang the doorbell.

I'll just ask to talk to her. Jake was sure that the lady in charge here—the Japanese lady—wouldn't mind. Was it so much to ask?

He could hear movement inside the building. Footsteps got louder, approaching the door. Looking up at the building, he could see the bedroom windows; they were all dark.

With a loud unlatching noise, the door swung open.

The Japanese lady stood there. She was smiling ferociously, wearing a dark gray business suit. Jake tried, but he couldn't remember her name.

"Yes?" the woman said expectantly.

"Hi," Jake said. "I'm Jake Montone; we met before, three nights ago. I'm Gaia Moore's friend."

"Yes?"

The woman didn't move. She didn't welcome him in, or step aside, or close the door. She just stood there, smiling tightly.

"Look, is she here? I need to talk to her."

"But you may not," the woman said firmly. "I'm sorry, that is the rule. It is too late; we have a curfew here."

"But—"

"And anyway, boys are not allowed. Here at Collingwood we have very strict regulations."

Jake took a deep breath. He was just so sick of this. He was so damn tired of all the obstacles he had to deal with all the time. It was just so easy to prevent a teenage boy from getting what he wanted. It was actually the reason he liked fighting. While sparring, you didn't have to take no for an answer.

Jake was reminded suddenly of Oliver Moore, Gaia's uncle. Now there was a man who could get things done. Who was old enough and smart enough to get results—who wouldn't let someone like this woman get in his way.

"Look," Jake said, in what he hoped was a sufficiently polite, reasonable tone. "Ma'am, I understand and respect that you've got rules. I think discipline's very important. And ordinarily I wouldn't dream of disrupting this place. But this is an unusual situation.

I'm not asking for the moon here. I'm just asking you to let me in for five minutes to talk to Gaia. And after that we'll—"

"Not allowed," the woman answered. She was shaking her head. "I am so sorry, but it is not allowed."

"But—"

"Good night," the woman said. She swung the door shut, and Jake was left standing atop the Collingwood steps in the dark.

Damn it.

Jake was disgusted with himself. He had walked all the way over here, all full of good ideas. . . and he'd accomplished nothing. He didn't even know if Gaia was *here* or not. He'd been completely useless.

"Pssst!"

Jake froze. He didn't move a muscle; he held his breath. There was no sound but the distant traffic and the drone of air conditioners. Plain New York sounds. He strained, trying to hear movement around him.

And he did. A rustling sound.

"Pssst!" The same voice again. This time with a clattering sound. *"Hey, you!"*

A female voice. Whispering.

Below him.

"Me?" Jake whispered quietly. He still hadn't moved. He was getting ready to turn around as fast as he could.

"Yes, you! Joe Stud. I have no idea what your name is." An endless giggle followed.

Jake thought he recognized the voice. It was hard to tell—the girl was whispering, after all—but there was something familiar about it.

"*Down here,*" the girl whispered. "*Under the stairs.*"

Under—?

Jake moved his head. And once he did, he saw light. Yellow light, spilling out onto Collingwood's stone facade. Slowly he stepped over to the side of the staircase and looked down toward the light. He moved carefully, ready to pull his head back in a moment if it was a trick of some kind.

Jake stared down past the edge of the staircase.

A small basement window was down there, along the side of the staircase. It was very small—you could easily miss it. A single bright yellow light shone inside the building.

And Jake could see a face looking up at him. A girl—a teenage girl—with very pretty features and long blond hair.

"*Hi.*" The girl smiled.

"*Hi.*" Jake was confused. He recognized the girl, though. He'd met her before, the night that Gaia had moved in. She had a strange, one-syllable name. . . *Zan*. That was it.

"*Get down here,*" Zan whispered.

Jake turned around and descended the stairs. He saw the way he had to vault over the low stone wall, landing on the concrete embankment that was sunk a few feet below sidewalk level. There were garbage cans that smelled of teriyaki, and a small iron grate. . . and a recessed door. Zan stepped through the door, her yellow hair strewn messily around her face, smiling at him.

He came closer.

"Hi, Zan," he said. "How are you?"

"Good," Zan said. She smiled a wide smile. "I am so ludicrously good right now, it's not even funny. What's your name again?"

"Jake."

"*Jake.*" She laughed. "God, yes, you are such a Jake. You are *all Jake.*" Zan grasped Jake's arms and began to run her hands down them slowly to test for firmness. Jake quickly slipped his arms from her grasp with an uncomfortable laugh.

"Oops." She smiled, leaning her face in closer. "*Inappropriate touching.* My bad—"

"Um, listen," Jake interrupted, taking a step back from Zan's *extremely friendly* energy. "I wonder if you can help me, Zan. I'm looking for Gaia Moore. Is she here?"

Zan took a good long look at Jake's face. "Jake," she announced, "I think it's important that you know: You are just an exquisite man. I mean it. Exquisite. *Magnifique.* I speak French." Zan laughed heartily at her own comic stylings. "Now, come on— what about me?" Zan stepped back, flipped her hair with a grand gesture, and froze in a supermodel position for Jake's approval. "Do you get my heat?" She grinned, just barely holding off her n e x t m a s - s i v e g i g g l e. "Are you feeling my heat, Jacob?" She swiped her fingers at him like cat claws, and then she pounced, throwing her arms around Jake's waist and moving way past the appropriate facial boundaries.

"Ho!" Jake uttered with deep discomfort. "You are so very clearly on Ecstasy right now." Once again he was forced to peel Zan's hands from his body.

"Yes, and you are so very clearly *not*," Zan said, toying with Jake as she dared him to guess where the next hand was coming from.

Jake was running out of patience fast. He would give it one more try and that would be that. "Look. . . is Gaia here? Gaia Moore. Moved in the other night. Messy blond hair, sweatshirt. You know."

"Yes, I *know*." Zan groaned. "I heard you the first time. Hey, I have the perfect solution here." She grinned again. "Why don't we go inside and wait for her, Jacob? I'll give you one hit now and then by the time Gaia gets home, we'll have an official party. Is that not genius?" Zan grasped Jake's hand and began to drag him farther inside. Jake had to use a considerable amount of force to put on the brakes.

"*No*," Jake complained. "No party, Zan. I don't go

near that stuff. And neither should you. Your brain is going to turn into—"

"No, Jacob, this is the *good stuff*," Zan insisted. "This is grade A, my friend. Straight from a lab in Cali. This is not that IV crap."

"What?"

"In. . . *vince*," Zan said. "You know—IV. The nasty stuff. That crap they're selling in the park. This isn't that. This is pure."

Jake froze for a moment.

Invince.

He started to flash back to voices in the darkness.

Oh God, my head. My freaking head.

It's dead Gaia night!

Jake began to remember. The cut on his chest. . . the bruise on his forehead.

"Zan," he said, "listen to me, okay? This is good Ecstasy, you said. . . not the IV stuff?"

"Best on the market," Zan assured him, tugging again to pull him inside. But Jake held his ground.

"Zan, what do you know about the bad stuff? The. . . Invince? Zan, come *on*, let go of me and *talk*. This is *important*."

Zan let out a frustrated groan and threw Jake's arm back at him. "God, what*ever*," she complained. "If you don't want to come up, *fine*. What do you think I am, the loneliest girl in the world or something?

225

Whatever." Zan swung around and headed back inside.

"No, Zan, wait. What about—?"

"She's gone," Zan grunted. "Your *girlfriend*. I have no idea where."

"With her father?"

"I have *no* idea. Get a *life*, Jacob." Zan shut the door behind her and flipped off the light.

"Wait, Zan!"

But that was that. She was gone. And Jake was alone in the dark, in the shadows next to the building.

What the hell?

Gaia wasn't here. Was she with her father? Zan hadn't told him.

But she had told him *something*. The kids who had attacked him and Gaia. . . he knew they had to be on something, he just hadn't been able to figure out *what*. Until now. Invince.

Jake was worried. More than ever, he wanted to know where Gaia was. Climbing carefully back onto the sidewalk, taking pains not to rattle the fragrant garbage cans, he tried to think of some way to find her. . . to make sure she was all right.

He couldn't think of a thing.

And he was convinced, more than ever, and for no reason he could name, that she wasn't all right at all. That she was in danger.

POINTLESS SMILE NUMBER TEN.

Completely in Love

That is what Ed and Kai had been reduced to on this, their big romantic date at La Métairie. Zero conversation and ten pointless silent smiles in a row.

But it was Ed's own fault and he knew it. He had decided to try and put as much energy into this gesture as he possibly could. He'd tried to arrange and execute the romantic date that Kai had been not so subtly pushing for in the last few days. But some part of him had always known. He'd known it was going to be a bust. He'd known it before he'd even made the reservation. And Kai knew it, too. Maybe she wasn't as quick to admit it. Maybe she didn't even want to admit it to herself, but this whole thing simply was not them. The restaurant was not them. Ed's stupid Gap sweater was not him, and Kai's little black cocktail dress wasn't her. The fancy food they'd ordered wasn't them; the dinner conversation they'd painstakingly tried to forge wasn't them. But really, it all came down to one simple fact that Ed was getting dangerously close to announcing yet again.

Romance was not them.

As much as he wanted it to be, as much as she wanted it to be, no amount of wanting could change the immutable nature of chemistry. And Ed's bizarre, part-cathartic/part-heartbreaking run-in with Gaia at the park had only driven that point home.

Ed knew why he'd pushed for the date tonight. He'd done it just to make a point to himself after seeing Gaia. To prove that he could be just as happy with Kai as Gaia could be with Jake. After all, if Gaia could make this mysterious "big change" for Jake, the least Ed could do was make dinner reservations with Kai.

But facts were facts. Ed could no longer be with Gaia, and he understood and respected that wholeheartedly. But that didn't change the fact that he was still completely in love with her. Apparently nothing was going to change that fact. Not for a very, very long time. Far longer than Kai or any other girl would or should be willing to wait.

And in truth, no matter what Kai said at dinner, Gaia was all Ed could think about. *The big change.* What the hell was she talking about? If he'd thought that Gaia gave two craps about her appearance, he would have sworn they were talking about something as shallow as breast implants or a nose job. But there was simply no way in hell that Gaia would ever be thinking for two seconds about such nonsense. And breast implants sure as hell were not going to remove all the endless tragedies in her life. So what, then? What on earth was she talking about?

But some part of Ed didn't even care what she was talking about. What he cared about was that of all the people she could have come to, she had come to him. And that meant something. It didn't have to mean anything about love or who she *really* wanted to be with or anything of that nature. It just meant that the good part of them hadn't gotten thrown out with the bad part. It meant that they had something of their own—something untouchable that would remain in spite of their need to move on.

"Ed. . ." Kai let out a long sigh. She had dispensed with her ebullient smiles at this point. "Ed, I was talking. I was talking again, and you have absolutely no idea what I was saying."

Ed's stomach twisted up into a knot. Not because he'd been caught in yet another moment of complete preoccupation, but more because it was just so unfair to Kai. Kai, who was this perfect little human being who could have a hundred guys doting on her day and night.

No more lies, Ed, don't you think?

He set his fork down on his plate, and he gave Kai what was probably the most honest and attentive look he'd given her in days. "You're right," he said. "You are right, Kai. I was not listening, and I have not *been* listening to you enough at all, and I would like to officially nominate myself as an asshole."

Kai laughed and shook her head. "No, Ed, you are not an asshole. This is my fault."

"What?"

Kai st her fork down, too, and gave Ed what was probably the most honest look she had given *him* in the last few days. "Ed, there's a little something we all tend to do every now and then, and it is called forcing the issue. I have been forcing the issue with you for a while now, and you are simply too kindhearted to make me stop. So I am going to stop. But for real this time. You need to get over Gaia, Ed. And I think you're a long way from that, don't you?"

It was not something Ed particularly wanted to say out loud. But then again, maybe it would do him some kind of good. "I do," he admitted.

"And don't you think that we make a great team as friends?"

"I do."

"And don't you think that it's time we left this stuffy restaurant?"

"I do." He laughed. Romance or not, they were sure as hell in sync.

Ed signaled for the check. "Do you want to go somewhere else? Maybe shoot some pool?"

Kai searched Ed's eyes a little more deeply. "I'm thinking we should just go our separate ways tonight," she said. "Maybe restart the friendship tomorrow? Possibly a Ping-Pong marathon. Don't you think we should call it a night?"

Ed smiled. "I do. Are you going to go home?"

"I don't know. I think I'm looking pretty cute.

There's a couple of parties I might hit over in the East Village. You?"

"I don't know," Ed replied truthfully. "It's been a pretty weird forty-eight hours for me. I think I'll probably just, you know, wander toward home. . . take a walk and try to clear my mind."

"Sounds nice," Kai said. "I'm heading east—you want to walk for a while?"

"Yeah. Yeah, I do," he said truthfully.

Ed paid the check and held the door for Kai as his one last romantic gesture for the evening. And then he and Kai were strolling side by side down the dark sidewalks. Ed could feel the weight lifting from his shoulders. He was finally here, on the other side of the conversation he'd been dreading. . . and he felt fine.

There wasn't any particular urgency to going home, Ed thought. And with Kai walking alongside him, Ed realized that there was still really only one place he could go to clear his mind and think. And whether it was the shining sun and the crowds in the daytime or the damp and quiet of the nighttime, he was sure it could still do him some good. So, with Kai walking agreeably beside him, he headed toward Washington Square Park.

I don't know how I could have become so stupid.

Stupid, ineffective, and slow. I don't know how that happened to me.

It's always the fate of strong people. When you're strong, everyone tries to rob you of your strength. It's just a natural process. If you expect it, if you see it coming. . . you can ward it off. You can guard against it.

That's what I've been forgetting to do. Keep people from robbing me of my strength. But I'm not going to forget any longer.

From now on, I'm going to take control. I'm going to make things happen the way they're supposed to, and nobody's going to stand in my way.

Why did it take me so long to get my network going? I waited *weeks* before doing that, when any idiot can see that it's the best way to get anything done. Within minutes I knew where Gaia was, thanks to my spies. And it would have taken the CIA much longer.

I should have killed those two
when they came to bother me. It
would have been easy. And then
Gaia would be safe.

Gaia—that wonderful, maddening
young woman. If I'd been just a
bit smarter, just a bit quicker,
I could have saved her from whatever dark fate she's chosen.
Whatever dangerous foolishness
they've talked her into.

If only, if only. It's like a
voice in my head that won't stop,
reprimanding me for my pathetic weakness. What was I doing writing her
letters? From the very beginning, I
should have been doing everything in
my power to keep her safe. Forget the
CIA, forget Tom: I'm the only one who
can do it. I'm the only one with the
strength of will.

God only knows what's happening to her right now. According
to my people, she's entered St.
Vincent's hospital and hasn't
come out. There's just no way of
knowing what's happening to her.

I'll get to the bottom of it.
And I'll destroy anyone who tries

to stop me—anyone who gets in my way. I'm not going to let my own weakness or confusion stop me from doing what's right.

How could Tom run away and leave his daughter so vulnerable, so unprotected? What kind of weak fool would do that?

But it's not his fault. He's the way God made him—there's no getting around that. He's always been confused since the day we were born. It's tragic, but it's the truth.

No, the failure's mine. I'm man enough to admit it. I let them get to me—all the naysayers and con men and fools. I let them bring me down.

But no more. Whoever is trying to stop me. . . trying to mess with Gaia. . . you may have won a round, but you'll lose the big fight. You have no *idea* who you're dealing with.

I'm not confused anymore. My head is clear. I've got my operatives back and my strength back, and now I'm going to make things right.

Watch out.

ALL SHE REALLY REMEMBERED FOR

Knives Outstretched

sure was counting to ten and waking up. Everything else was foggy.

She remembered Dr. Ulrich keeping her at ease as they prepped her for examination and treatment. She had been compelled to keep reminding him that she did not *need* to be kept at ease. Though hopefully that was all going to change now. . . .

The doctor had spent a fair amount of time trying to describe the specifics of the treatment to her as he worked, but they had already begun administering the initial anesthetic, so she could really only recall bits and pieces.

The most she could gather in her memory was that they had required a massive sampling of her genetic material. She remembered the seemingly endless pricks of needles from various locations on her body. Then, as best as she could understand it, once they had made the genetic corrections to the samples, they would then combine that corrected material with something Dr. Ulrich called an adenovirus. The corrected material was reintroduced to her bloodstream with an injection of that adenovirus, which would act as a superfast carrier and start a chain reaction of genetic regeneration. There was clearly much more to it than that, but Gaia couldn't possibly have understood every aspect of it. In this rare case, she accepted the fact that she was simply a patient. A very important patient, yes, but still, just a patient. A patient with a lot of fantasy-level hopes and dreams.

And there had been plenty of time to dream. Twenty-four hours. That was how long she had stayed unconscious while they waited for the treatment to take. And when she awoke, Dr. Ulrich and his staff had been there, waiting for her. She had felt surprisingly refreshed upon waking, not sluggish at all, almost like waking up from a good night's sleep. It hadn't taken long before she was dressed and signing off on all the necessary release forms.

They had insisted on putting her in a taxicab, and she had agreed and promised to go straight home and go to sleep. . . but after she'd traveled ten blocks, she'd changed her mind, asked the cab to stop, and started walking. She couldn't help it; she just had to be outside, experiencing this new sensation completely. A voice in her head told her that she had just lied again. . . and that it was becoming a bad habit. But she ignored it.

And now, as she walked home through the West Village, she could hear Dr. Ulrich's intelligent voice echoing through her head. His parting statement was really the only thing that mattered to Gaia now:

If the treatment has taken, expect an indication

within the next hour or less. But if the treatment has not taken now, then I'm afraid it never will.

Gaia was doing her best to walk the streets prepared for both eventualities. She had to prepare herself for the very real possibility that the entire procedure had been futile and that she would officially be consigned to the fearless life she had come to know and despise. But much, much more importantly than that, she was trying to prepare herself for the other possibility—the very legitimate possibility that at any moment her new life would begin.

So she was testing. Testing in every way she could think of as she passed Waverly Place heading down Seventh Avenue.

What might scare her? Who might scare her? What would be the first indication if and when it hit? She remembered the feelings of absolute horror she'd had after Loki had given her that injection, but that hadn't been fear. Not really. That had been practically dementia and schizophrenia and paranoia, complete with deadly fever hallucinations and irrational terrors that had left her nearly paralyzed. No, now she was looking for the *real* thing—the feelings and behaviors she'd spent her entire life understanding only by observation. The way a person's shoulders would jerk upward when a loud noise took them by surprise. The way a girl would screech at the top of her lungs when a cat jumped across the screen in a horror movie. The way she'd seen people shiver and chatter and cower and duck. And even the `very real screams` she'd heard in New York City. When it wasn't a movie. When the circumstances were painfully real. She was constantly checking her body and her mind for any of it. Any of that stuff that had never made a stitch of sense to her. She had even seriously considered running smack into the middle of moving traffic just to see what would happen—to see whether she would stiffen up like a deer in headlights or dive desperately for the curb. But she wasn't stupid. It was her fearlessness she had hoped to remove. Not her intelligence.

By the time she'd begun to cross Bleecker Street on her way to the boardinghouse, she was having some serious and extremely depressing doubts. Loud noises hadn't done a thing to her. And neither had traffic, and neither had her continuous attempts to take the darkest and seediest streets possible. She was beginning to feel like only two possibilities remained. Either the treatment had failed, or else life was just not particularly scary. But judging from what she'd heard from most of the human race, the latter did not seem all that likely.

As her depression really kicked in, she dropped down on one of the empty benches in the park and began to simmer.

All that trouble. All that goddamn trouble for nothing. The talks with Dr. Ulrich, the talks with Ed and Chris, the entire procedure, and all for *what*? For this. Another wasted fearless night in the not remotely frightening dark shadows of Washington Square Park? The trees loomed and swayed in the breeze just like they always had. The wind blew the leaves along the empty paths just like it always had. Everything was miserably and exactly as it always was and as it always would be. What the hell was the point?

But the point, it turned out, was a giggle. Not even the giggle so much as what happened when Gaia heard the giggle.

It was her shoulders. Her shoulders had jerked. They had *jerked*—so slightly upward that the average person probably wouldn't have even noticed it. But Gaia noticed it. She noticed it because it was the first time in her life that it had ever happened.

It's happening. Jesus, it's actually happening.

Gaia turned behind her and tried to see where the giggle had come from. But she could see nothing. She could only hear them. It was a "them" now. The giggle had turned into two and then three—giggles growing louder and louder but from no discernable place— either the trees or the bushes, she couldn't tell. But they were getting closer.

And then her chest began to tighten. And her spine began to stiffen. And it suddenly became very difficult to swallow, because her mouth was growing drier and drier by the second.

My God, it's really happening.

She wasn't imagining it. She was sure of it. She wasn't trying to force the symptoms of fear. She didn't need to force them. They were beginning to unload on her like heavy machinery. And as sick and as odd as they were beginning to make her feel, Gaia was in such a twisted state that she actually found herself wanting to dole out thanks. She wanted to thank Dr. Ulrich and the Rodkes, especially Chris. And Ed, too, for talking her through that very last step. Christ, it was like she had won an award or something. The award of being dry mouthed and ill at ease. The award of having her heart race far and beyond any kind of comfort level. The award of `feeling like her own death was actually imminent` if she didn't do something to make her stiffened limbs move. At this one moment, here at the very beginning of this new life, Gaia was well aware of the fact that she was a sick, sick puppy, elated to be terrified, delighted to be feeling ill with panic, overwhelmed with joy at how deeply joyless it was to be stuck in the middle of Washington Square Park, alone and after dark and in serious, serious trouble. But to *know* it. To really feel it. To actually feel that she was utterly and completely screwed.

Gaia's emotions began to diverge into a chaotic heap, pulling her head in so many directions that it felt like a massive tug-of-war inside her skull. On the one hand, there was the *rush*. The rush of fear. It was enormous and palpable. The rush of feeling *real*, feeling totally, 100 percent *human*. Not to mention the glorious and perfect sense of beginning something. Something truly new. Something she had been dreaming about and hopelessly praying for year after year.

But on the other hand. . . there was the why—the *reason* that these delicious new symptoms were taking control of her body. She knew those giggles. She knew them far too well. She knew them so well that her shoulders had recognized them even before she had.

Them. The freakish skinheads from hell. Those were their giggles. The sound was unmistakable. And now Gaia was a sitting duck right in the middle of their little trap. And her mind had suddenly turned to one very essential question: Just what would these "wonderful" new symptoms do to her fighting skills? How would they affect her defenses? What was it like to fight when your body and a huge portion of your brain were begging you to run? Not just begging, but *ordering*. Her entire being was ordering her to hit the road, here and now, before any of those psychotic assholes took another step toward her.

But she had left herself with no more time to think about it, no more time to wonder. Because they had already rolled out of the bushes and begun to converge on her bench with the same wild-eyed vengeance that she'd seen the last time. The test had already begun. And she already despised the results.

Move, goddamn it, move.

"We've got her all to ourselves this time!" one of them howled. Gaia recognized him immediately. The swastika earring dangling from his left ear, the huge gash on his arm that he'd inflicted all by himself.

His first knife swipe cut off a swatch of her hair, and another set of brand-new symptoms erupted. A gasp fell from her lips. Shivers shot through each of her legs, making them wobbly and unsure. She couldn't even take the time to see how many of them there were because her eyes were darting in all directions from panic. Fights had always seemed like slow motion to Gaia. There had always been plenty of time to plan, to organize, to concentrate. Now it was just the opposite. Everything felt sped up. Too fast to keep track of anything, no time to focus on anything other than her pathetically wobbly legs.

And now there was a new voice screaming in her head. A voice she had never heard before. And its message was simple.

You're dead. Jesus Christ, you are going to die here tonight. There is no doubt about it. You don't have a chance in hell.

She was learning. She was learning fast. A new lesson every second. Fear and pessimism. . . they were somehow connected. She had to keep reminding herself what she was capable of. Because she kept forgetting. The closer their knives got, the more she seemed to forget her ability to dodge them—to do a hell of a lot more than dodge them. For Christ's sake, she was still the same *person*—wasn't she?

She rocketed through three quick forward rolls just to buy herself a little time, a little distance. But they were closing in so fast.

"Feel the power, bitch!" They were chanting it over and over. "Feel the power of God!"

"I'm gonna mark this bitch with an *X*!" one of them howled. "I'm gonna scratch a big fat *X* right through this bitch's back!"

The mob howled their support as they all gave in to fits of giddy laughter, storming toward her with their knives outstretched.

Focus, goddamn it! Please, Gaia. Focus.

Latest lesson: Fear could leave a girl actually pleading with herself.

The knife nearly cut her chest straight down the middle, but she managed to grab her assailant's wrist first, twisting his arm straight out of its socket and then flipping him flat on his back. But the next knife was already coming down from the left.

"No!" Gaia screamed. It had just flown out of her mouth—this totally involuntary plea for her life.

She crammed her knee sharply into his groin and then snapped a hard back kick to his jaw that flattened him out. But she was already out of juice, and she could feel it.

Lesson number six: Fear saps every ounce of energy that you should have had on reserve.

And so she began to back away as they advanced. She *had* to or she was dead. A backward roll and another backward roll.

"Oh, man, look at the Gaia bitch!" the leader cackled. "Look who's afraid now. We are freaking supermen, and look who's turned into a plain old girlie bitch."

"*X!*" that asshole howled again. "I gotta have it. I've gotta see a bloody *X* on this bitch." He started to pick up speed, driving toward her. But Gaia didn't have it in her to take him down. Not anymore. No way. She'd make a mistake now—she'd screw it up, she was sure of it. So she did all she had left in her to do. She dove fast and hard into the bushes, landing on her hands and knees in the brush and searching for a safe place to hide.

"Oh, man, come *on.*" The *X* man laughed. "It's gonna be like *that* now?"

She crawled through the bushes, gasping for air. Their laughter only grew louder and louder as they stomped around on all sides, trying to spot her. She dropped flat to the ground with her face nearly in the dirt and tried to catch her breath and make a plan. What the hell was she going to do now? She was exhausted, disoriented, and freaked out of her mind. How the hell was she going to take out the *X* man before he took her out? There was no way. There was no way she could do it.

And then, quite suddenly, with her nose stuck in

the dirt and the sweat pouring down her face, Gaia had an epiphany. An honest-to-God revelation.

She didn't have to do this anymore.

She was just a girl now. Just a normal, fearful, real live girl. She didn't want to fight anymore. That was the entire point. Her entire fearless life had boiled down to fight after fight after fight. It had been all she had. It had been the only thing that gave her any pleasure. But that was all going to change now. Let the NYPD deal with the *X* man. That's what they were here for: to protect the normal everyday citizens like Gaia Moore.

The *X* man was no longer her responsibility. She was not responsible for every two-bit scumbag and drugged-out skinhead in New York City. She was out. She was finally out. Out of the fighting game. Out of the vigilante justice game. She was free. Free to fall in love and have a relationship and a family like everybody else. Free to run for her goddamn life. Just like everybody else.

And that was just what she did. She took off with every ounce of strength and speed she had in her. She ran for her life. The life that she was finally starting to believe she could have.

And as she stomped her way up the steps of the boardinghouse and found her way to her bed, Gaia knew that she would always remember this night. She'd remember it as the night that new Gaia was officially born.

IT WAS MAGIC. THERE WAS NO
other way to put it.

Averted Eyes

A beautiful, magical New York morning. The air was sparkling clear. The busy street was filled with hurrying pedestrians and honking taxicabs and huge delivery trucks and all the wonderful bits and pieces of Manhattan life.

Gaia walked toward school, transported. She felt wonderful. There was no other way to put it. The feeling running through her was like an electric current—it reminded her of being a little girl, when her mother was alive. That special feeling of being a young child, of wanting to burst into song or start running or skipping for no reason except that you felt like it.

I'm normal, she told herself. *I'm complete.*

Gaia crossed Sixth Avenue and made her way east toward the Village School. The blue sky was as clear and bright as a picture postcard. Gaia wanted to stop and greet everyone she saw and thank them for being part of her wonderful morning.

She had fear.

It was like a missing musical note had been added, and now the symphony was complete. *This* was what it was like for everyone else. She still remembered the exquisite sensation the night before when those assholes had attacked. That incredible, terrible moment when she'd realized that she was *afraid*. The pain of the fear had been like a spice added to the joy she'd felt.

Gaia turned the last street corner and saw the front of the Village School. The crowd in front of the place seemed unusually light, but then, she was early. She was actually early to school—imagine that.

Gaia had surprised the hell out of Suko that morning. She'd woken up early, showered and dressed, and then practically galloped downstairs. She'd had breakfast at Collingwood rather than just buying a bagel on her way to school. Philip had been delighted, serving her eggs and coffee with great flourishes.

And now here she was, at school—and Gaia knew exactly what she was going to do.

She was going to walk into the building. Then she was going to play her new game—the game where she tried to pick Jake out of the crowd.

The dark hair: check. The smooth olive skin: check. And step three—the confident swagger. She was going to walk right up to him and grab his shoulder, and when he turned around, she was going to kiss him full on the lips, right there in front of everyone. And then she was going to hug him as hard as she could and murmur into his ear that she was sorry, so sorry, so terribly sorry that she'd been so difficult. . . but that all of that was over now. Everything had changed for her. . . and for them.

Gaia was sure of it. It was all different, in the best

possible way. Now, *finally*, she could have that talk with Jake. She *wanted* to have that talk. She wanted him to ask lots of questions so that she could say yes to each of them and watch his face as she did it.

She couldn't wait.

Gaia bashed through the front door of the school, practically singing with excitement. She was looking for anyone she knew. Especially Chris. So she could make a point of thanking him for what he'd done for her.

Her eyes adjusted to the relative darkness as the big doors swung shut behind her. It was strange: she'd been expecting to hear the usual dull roar of high school voices, the sound tumbling toward her, assaulting her eardrums as it did every morning.

But she didn't hear anything.

It was like walking into a library or a church.

Now Gaia's eyes had fully adjusted to the darkness, and she realized something else.

Nobody was moving.

There were students and teachers. . . and they were all standing there. Not moving. Not speaking. Not doing anything. . . just standing there. Even the people she didn't know, had never spoken to.

Looking at Gaia.

That wasn't quite it. They were gazing at her and then quickly looking away. As if they couldn't bring themselves to make eye contact.

What. . . ?

Gaia was confused. It was like a dream, one of those dreams where you enter a familiar place and somehow it's become strange.

Gaia walked forward into the school. The few people in the lobby kept avoiding her gaze.

What's going on? What is this?

Unless Gaia was mistaken, the averted eyes weren't random. It was her, specifically. It really seemed like there was something about Gaia Moore that made them not want to look.

And Gaia was scared.

There was nothing remotely pleasurable about it. Not this time. There was no novelty, no delighted surprise. Just. . . this feeling. This terrible feeling in the pit of her stomach that spread like a cold, dark shadow across her body. It made her feel weak. It made her feel sick.

It was fear.

And it was bad. *Can I change my mind?* Gaia thought for a second. Just for a second, but she was aware of having the thought. `Walking like a ghost` through the school lobby as everyone in the room stood by the lockers and avoided her eyes, Gaia wondered if maybe she had made some kind of mistake. . . if maybe, just maybe, she could take it back.

I want to wake up, Gaia thought crazily. She knew she wasn't sleeping, but nevertheless, that was how she felt. *Okay, I want to wake up now. This isn't funny. I want things back the way they're supposed to be.*

And then she saw him.

Thick dark hair. Olive skin.

Jake.

He saw her at the same time. And she couldn't believe what she saw in his face.

Jake looked terrible. He looked awful.

All of them, Gaia realized, looking around at all the silent people who wouldn't look back at them. *They all look bad.*

Jake came toward her and she thought the stricken look on his face would break her heart. Her fear was so intense that it nearly made her faint. She didn't feel like she was starting a great new life. She felt like she was trapped in some kind of bad dream she didn't understand.

Jake grabbed her and hugged her hard.

Gaia felt a hand on her shoulder. She pulled away from Jake, and looked over. . . and saw Tannie Deegan.

Tannie was crying. And holding Gaia's shoulder like she was drowning.

"What. . . ?" Gaia could barely make her throat work. The fear was paralyzing, stupefying. She managed to clear her throat and try again. She stared up at Jake's solemn face. "What is it? What happened?"

And when Jake replied, the next two words `went through Gaia like a spear.`

"It's Ed," Jake rasped. "Ed Fargo. Ed and Kai."

And he hugged her again.

"What?" Gaia begged. She could hear her own voice breaking. "What? Jake, please. . . tell me. . . ."

"They got attacked. Last night, by those. . . by those kids. Those kids on that damn Invince."

What?

Gaia was sure she'd misheard. Because if not—if she'd heard correctly— "What's Invince?" she croaked.

"The bad drug," Jake went on. "Gaia, I found out last night. . . ."

"*What about Ed?*" Gaia begged. The fear was overwhelming now. It was amazing to her that she'd ever been so crazy as to ask for this: this terrible, crushing, horrible feeling that made her want to curl up on the floor and die. "Please, Jake—what happened to Ed?"

"He's in the hospital," Jake said. "He's in critical condition at the hospital. And one of them. . . one of those sick bastards. . . They cut them, Gaia. They cut him bad. In his back. Someone slashed a freaking *X* in his back. . . ."

Jake's words were like bullets tearing through the fog of fear, and Gaia couldn't make them stop.

The kids.

The ones she hadn't fought, hadn't stopped.

"Kai's over the worst of it. She got a transfusion, and there's no scarring, but. . . but they don't know if Ed's going to make it," Tannie whispered. She was clutching Gaia now. "His mother's there. They just announced that they're closing the school for the day. Everyone's going home."

Gaia realized she was going to scream. She wondered vaguely if she'd ever done it before. She realized that she probably hadn't. Jake was clutching her, holding her up, and then Gaia realized that she had it wrong. She wasn't going to scream. She was going to faint. Just like she used to after fighting, back when she was fearless.

Gaia thought of Ed and Kai, lying in hospital beds, slashed in God knew how many places. It was unbearable. She wanted to go back in time; she wanted, more than she'd ever wanted anything in her life, to fix it, to make it all right. To take it back. But there was no way to do it. Gaia saw the world begin to fade as Jake's arms held her, and then the world grew dark and she faded into blackness.

Ed. . . Kai. . . I'm sorry. . . .

FIELD REPORT: OPERATION CONCLUDED

Rowan, J., and Morrow, P., reporting

Following interviews with Oliver Moore, aka Loki (see attached file 45071-a), and Heather Gannis (see attached file 31), operatives Rowan and Morrow have concluded their investigation into the genetic serum code named BLUEBELL.

The investigation has revealed several conclusive facts. The BLUEBELL serum did in fact exist; it was created under the supervision of Oliver Moore, aka Loki; it was administered to Heather Gannis and to Gaia Moore (see attached files 61, 63, 63-A, 72); it caused different effects in these two test subjects.

Heather Gannis's blindness, as theorized, is a side effect of the BLUE-BELL virus's genetic manipulation.

However, before the blindness set in, Heather Gannis did experience a sustained period of "fearlessness." This suggests that the BLUEBELL virus functioned as an "accelerator," as has been discussed by geneticist Karl Ulrich (see attached file 202) and other scientists.

More importantly, the interviews have confirmed that all previously available information regarding the BLUEBELL virus was correct, as were the theories concerning the unique genetic composition of Gaia Moore. This seventeen-year-old girl does not possess the "fear gene," which means that her assimilation of the BLUEBELL virus (without going blind) was successful.

This information has been provided to management under separate cover; although details have not been revealed, it appears that this information has been well used. Gaia Moore has been targeted and coerced into cooperation, and the procedure has been completed. According to division reports, test samples will be ready shortly and the countdown has begun.

Attempts by Moore and Gannis to warn others of our activities have failed.

Stage one of the program is concluded; it may be regarded as a complete success. Stage two is now under way.

END

Read an excerpt from the
latest book in the hot
new series

SAMURAI GIRL

BOOK FIVE

THE
BOOK
OF THE
FLAME

1

"Shut up. And tell your boyfriend to shut up, too," Pablo snapped.

I clamped my mouth shut and looked over at Hiro, who sat next to me in the backseat of the black sedan. An ugly-looking bruise was spreading across Hiro's left cheek (those beautiful cheekbones!) and blood trickled down his forehead. His lower lip was swollen, and his jeans were covered in dirt and more blood. And if the pain that racked my body was any sign, I didn't look much better myself. We'd just crossed the Mexican border into California (thanks to the handful of cash I'd seen Pablo cram into the customs officer's pocket), and I had no idea where we were headed.

Hiro shook his head at me slowly.

"Do what he says," he mouthed, and I nodded, trying to stop the swell of tears I felt stinging my eyes. It was unbearable to think that I might be leading Hiro to his death. This was my fight, my battle, and these thugs, whoever they were, wanted me, not him. Now, for the first time since my long journey had begun, I couldn't see a way out. We were going almost a hundred miles an hour through the California desert. My hands were tightly bound behind my back, with a rope connecting them to my ankles, which were also bound. I felt like a cow being led to the slaughter, helpless and doomed.

I was propped up awkwardly against Hiro, unable to sit up straight. After a few minutes I felt him writhing against me. "Are you hurt?" I whispered. Hiro shook his head but kept squirming. I looked nervously toward the front seat, where Pablo sat puffing a huge cigar and driving way too fast. It was hard to believe that when Teddy had introduced me to Pablo back in Vegas, I hadn't immediately sensed what a dangerous guy he was—as if the blingy jewelry and greased-back hair weren't enough, he had a mouthful of gold teeth. I prayed he and his cohort wouldn't turn around.

I glanced back at Hiro. The veins on his neck stuck out from the effort he was making not to move as he worked at the cord around his wrists. I held my breath right along with him, willing Pablo and Co. not to look. I wasn't sure if "escape artist" was on Hiro's list of abilities, but I hoped so.

Hiro gave a tight-lipped smile. I looked down. The ropes holding him had gone slack. He'd wriggled his way out.

My heart leapt. Maybe this wasn't the end. Hiro motioned with his eyes that I should maneuver into a position where he

3

could work on the knots that bound me without being seen. I scooted around in the seat, focused all the time on Pablo and his buddy, who both seemed to be intent on celebrating with their nasty-smelling cigars. In between puffs they growled at each other in Spanish, and the unknown thug, who had a bristling mustache that couldn't hide the ugly scar slashing across his lip and down his jawline, kept gesturing with his gun for emphasis.

In a few moments I was free. I resisted the urge to stretch my arms and legs—or to hurl myself into Hiro's arms, to hug him and tell him I was sorry for this, for all of this. As if in answer to my thoughts, the car jolted without warning, throwing Hiro against me.

"Your mission is to achieve heightened perception," he whispered in my ear. "You must be aware of everything around you. That's the only way you're going to make it."

"What's going on back there? Didn't I tell you to shut up?" Mustache (as I'd come to think of him) turned around and waved his gun at us. My heart pounded as I cringed back against the seat. Having a gun shoved in your face in real life is freaking scary. Any bravery you might have on top just oozes right out of you. And I was terrified he'd notice that we were no longer tied up.

"I just wanted to make sure she was okay," Hiro said, his voice calm.

"You can't help your little girlfriend anymore," Mustache leered, his grin twisted and grotesque. "Just do as you're told."

5

He turned around, and Hiro gave me a look that said, "Simmer down." I stared out the window into the glaring heat.

I had a lot of work to do. First I had to pull myself out of my body to try to forget about the pain and stiffness that always set in after a fight. Then I had to clear my head of the images—the gang of mystery men bursting into our hotel room, the thud and thunk of the bone-crushing kicks and punches, the sight of Teddy sliding down to the ground, his back covered in blood. . . .

I squeezed my eyes shut, as if that could help drive the images away. I'd seen Teddy slump to the floor, bloody and broken, and when Pablo and his gang finally had beaten us into submission and dragged us from the motel room, I'd noticed smears of blood on the low wall by the open window. Whether Teddy had jumped or been thrown, I didn't know. But he had died alone. I'd looked for his body on our way out of the building, but it was already gone, probably dragged off by one of Pablo's henchmen.

There was no question in my mind that I was responsible. When I'd run into Teddy in Vegas, I'd been so happy to see someone I felt was on my side, who really *knew* my story, that I'd overlooked the dangers of us being seen together. Even though I believed his family, the Yukemuras (who were yakuza—Japanese mafia, just like mine, as I'd recently discovered), were still after me, and even though I knew that Teddy was involved with Colombian drug runners . . . Not exactly the most savory set of circumstances.

6

I'd tried not to think about it. But I'd agreed to flee Vegas with him because I thought Hiro had abandoned me. I'd used Teddy. He was no innocent, but his heart was certainly in the right place. And now he was gone. Just like that. I felt like such a stupid idiot. What had I planned to tell him when the three of us eventually made it to Europe, like we'd planned? *"Thanks a bunch, Teddy! I know you loved me and saved my life, but I want to be with Hiro now! See ya!"* Stupid.

I tried to untangle the thoughts teeming in my head, but it seemed like as soon as I put one to rest, another jumped to fill its place—and my brain just kept digging deeper. The first images that floated to the surface were of my father, lying in a coma in Japan, and my dead brother, Ohiko—I was still no closer to finding out who wanted my family dead. I imagined my father lying in a crisp white hospital bed, my stepmother, Mieko, at his side. Then I wondered again about her involvement in all that had happened, and my mind lingered on the confrontation I'd had with Marcus and his gangbangers on a subway platform in L.A. *"Your step-mother says hello,"* he'd said.

I squeezed my eyes tightly shut and let my mind drift past that memory and on to the next. Cheryl, my only friend in L.A., popped up, pink-streaked hair and all. For all I knew, she was dead now, too, trapped in a fire that had been set for me. I'd hurt all the people who'd tried to help me, I realized. It hurt too much to think about. . . . I pushed the images away and let a picture of Hiro take their place. I

7

thought of the moment I found out he felt the same way about me as I did about him—and how, in order to admit it, he'd had to break Karen's heart.

Guilt, fear, shame, love, pain—so many feelings clogging up the works. I tried every technique in the book, first visualizing bundling up my thoughts into a neat package and hurling them out the car window into the dusty desert, then imagining each one floating up out of the top of my head, leaving my mind a clean, empty slate. After what felt like forever, I managed to clear a tiny corner of my head. *Think, Heaven, think,* I told myself. *What exists around you? What can you feel? Who are the people holding you prisoner? Is there anything in the car you can use as a weapon? And most important, how can you and Hiro get yourselves out of this?*

A gentle tap on my ankle brought me back to reality. Hiro gave me a meaningful look and nodded slightly out the rear window. A silver SUV was behind us. I watched the SUV follow our sedan into a passing lane, then move smoothly back behind us when we switched lanes again.

We were being followed. I looked at Hiro and raised my eyebrows. So much for my powers of perception—I hadn't even noticed.

"We're being followed," Hiro said in a loud, clear voice.

Mustache turned around, and the SUV simultaneously slipped back into the stream of traffic, hiding itself. "Don't be a smartass," Mustache rumbled.

"Look for yourself," Hiro said steadily.

Mustache flipped around in his seat and I heard the click of his knife opening before I saw the flash of metal held to Hiro's throat. I gasped. Hiro stared silently at Mustache without moving. I started to tremble and readied myself to intervene if Mustache went too far. Was he for real? Or was he just trying to scare us?

"*Que estas haciendo? Nos son inútiles si son muertos,*" Pablo barked. Mustache looked irritated, but he clicked his knife shut and turned around.

"You're right," he said in his thickly accented English. "They're not worth anything dead. That comes later." I couldn't see his face, but something told me he was smiling.

I caught my breath and concentrated on the SUV that was so clearly tailing us. If the thugs in the front seat were sent by the Yukemuras, as I'd thought when they first busted into the hotel room with Teddy in tow, then who the hell was following us? I watched Mustache stare into the rear- and side-view mirrors; then he and Pablo started arguing again. Suddenly Mustache flipped around and grabbed my ponytail, yanking my head back.

"Who are they?" he yelled, his funky, stinking breath washing over my face. I shrank back against the hot leather seat, less to get away from the smell (although believe me, I wanted to) than to keep my hands and ankles hidden. I saw Hiro's face grow tight. I knew he'd lash out if he could, but he couldn't risk giving us away—our freedom was our one advantage, however small. I took a deep breath and

9

tried to resist the pain and the urge to kick Mustache's butt.

"I don't know," I yelped, trying to sound deferential and clueless. "I really don't!" Actually, it wasn't hard—even though I wasn't the best actress, I really hadn't the slightest clue where all this was headed. But I knew it was nowhere good.

The car lurched, and Mustache lost his hold on my hair. I took the opportunity to slink out from under his grip.

"Shit!" yelled Mustache, dropping heavily back into the front seat.

"Are they better than these guys or worse?" I asked Hiro in Japanese.

"Callate!" Mustache roared. "How many times do I have to tell you to keep your mouths shut?" The engine groaned as Pablo floored the gas. Hiro and I were thrown back against our seats—full-on chase mode. The silver SUV had given up any attempt to hide itself, and soon it clung within inches of the sedan, tailgating us so close that eventually its front bumper was tapping against our back one. The sedan shuddered, and I went rigid.

"Kangaete miru na," Hiro said. "Don't think about it. Just concentrate on what you see. Stay alert." He grabbed my hand and squeezed. I held my breath as we weaved in and out of lanes, trying to lose the SUV. Green highway signs flipped by, and in just minutes we were on the outskirts of San Diego. My heart leapt into my throat as we veered into another lane, and a red Volkswagen Bug

10

slammed on its horn and its brakes in an attempt to avoid us. We slipped by untouched, but the Bug wasn't so lucky. A horrifying screech split the air, followed by the sound of metal crunching metal, and when I looked back, the Bug was lying on its side, sliding down the highway. Cars slowed behind the accident, but the SUV shot through like a silver dart. I almost covered my eyes before I remembered that my hands were supposedly tied.

With a sudden wrench the sedan flew across four lanes in a flurry of honking, and we careened onto an exit ramp, kicking up a stream of orange utility cones in our wake. I screamed as we blew through a stoplight at the bottom of the ramp, narrowly missing a white convertible and leaving another fender-bender pileup behind us. Two teenagers in baggy pants jumped out of the way as we squealed around a corner, and we narrowly avoided crashing into a long median planted with palm trees. I was in the grip of a fear I had never known—death was staring us in the face, and there was nothing we could do about it. Our fate was out of our hands, which was so much worse than just being in a fight—at least then you could fight back. I looked down and saw that I had dug my nails into Hiro's hand, leaving vivid red crescents on his tan skin. Was this how we were going to go? I prayed we wouldn't take any innocent pedestrians down with us.

With a sickening lurch the sedan hopped a curb and spun out onto a faded green lawn. Within seconds Pablo had whirled the car around and bashed into the SUV, which was trying to block us in on the dead-end street.

"*Pendejo!*" Pablo yelled, twisting the steering wheel around as far as it would go. We screeched by the SUV and turned right.

A one-way street. And we were going the wrong way.

"Put on your seat belt!" I yelled to Hiro over the wind whistling in through the open windows and the approaching sounds of sirens. It was certainly *not* the time to worry about Mustache and friend finding out we were no longer tied. Horns blared as car after car came right at us before veering aside—the world's deadliest game of chicken. I snapped my seat belt in place and looked at Hiro for the last time. We were doing eighty on a residential street. Hiro stared into my eyes.

"I love you, Heaven Kogo," he said.

I grabbed his hand. "Yes," I answered, then looked away. I don't know why I said it, why I ignored the voice in my head that chanted, *I love you too, I love you, I love you.* The words wouldn't come. I was filled with a deep sadness at the prospect of our deaths. I felt an overwhelming tenderness for Hiro, for myself, for *life*. A red light loomed ahead. We weren't slowing down. As we crossed the intersection, I saw a car heading straight for us.

And then the car hit.

Will Heaven make it? Read Samurai Girl #5,
The Book of the Flame
Available now